I grabbed my backpack and slipped it over my shoulder. Then I reached for my cap.

It wasn't there.

I dug my hand deeper into the top shelf of my locker.

Nope.

I got up on my toes and stuck my face in. No cap.

I felt needle pricks of panic down my spine.

LUCKY CAP

Patrick Jennings

EGMONT
USA
NEW YORK

EGMONT

We bring stories to life

First published by Egmont USA, 2011
This paperback edition published by Egmont USA, 2012
443 Park Avenue South, Suite 806
New York, NY 10016

1 3 5 7 9 8 6 4 2

www.egmontusa.com
www.patrickjennings.com

THE LIBRARY OF CONGRESS HAS CATALOGED THE HARDCOVER EDITION AS FOLLOWS:

Jennings, Patrick.
Lucky cap / Patrick Jennings.
p. cm.
Summary: Enzo starts middle school after an amazing summer trip with his father, a new
manager at a popular sporting goods company, with a prototype baseball cap that seems
to bring Enzo popularity and success.
ISBN 978-1-60684-054-2 (hardcover) – ISBN 978-1-60684-275-1 (electronic book)
[1. Conduct of life—Fiction. 2. Popularity—Fiction. 3. Caps (Headgear)—Fiction. 4. Middle
schools—Fiction. 5. Schools—Fiction.] I. Title.
PZ7.J4298715Lu2011
[Fic]—dc22
2010051413

Paperback ISBN 978-1-60684-306-2

Book design by Arlene Goldberg

Printed in the United States of America

**Dedicated to the
Writers of the Cave**

Contents

*That's right, no Chapter 13. Details later. —Enzo

LUCKY CAP

1. The End of the Most Amazingest Trip in the History of Time

"We're heading home after checkout, Enzo," Dad told me one morning in the restaurant of a Sacramento hotel as I was busy scarfing down French toast stuffed with cheese and drenched in maple syrup.

I will never eat stuffed French toast again.

The trip was over? How did this happen? All six weeks couldn't possibly have come and gone so fast. Time is so unfair. It whizzes by when you're having the most incredible fun of your life, then drags when you're totally miserable, like, say, when you're stuck at the wedding of people you're not even sure you know.

Dad and his boss, Evan, set their hands on my shoulders, to steady me. I was feeling pretty wobbly. Then they took turns tousling my hair. I hate having my hair tousled.

"Don't!" I whined like a little kid, and pushed their hands away.

Evan laughed. "Don't take it so hard. Even the most awesome things have to come to an end sooner or later."

I seethed.

"We'll always have our memories," Dad said.

I scowled.

"And don't forget the killer sportswear!" added Evan.

"I can't tell you how great it was getting to spend so much time with you." This was Dad. They were tag-teaming me with bright sides. I bet they discussed how to handle me beforehand.

"Ditto that." (Evan.) "You're a great kid, Lorenzo Harpold. I hope I have a son like you some day."

"We're closer than ever." (Dad.)

"What an awesome, awesome adventure!" (Evan.)

"Totally!" (Dad.)

"You said it yourself, Enz:'The most amazingest trip in the history of time!'" (Evan.)

Sure, every word of it was all true, but it wasn't helping. How could it? I wasn't just disappointed or let down or sad. I was crushed. Like, by a steamroller.

Hearing that being crushed by a steamroller is bad, but you'll always have your memories, is not helpful.

The end of the trip was a steamroller.

"Well," Dad said, glancing at his watch, "we'd better get going."

Evan nodded and they both scooted out of the elbow-macaroni-shaped booth, leaving me behind, in the middle of the elbow, in shock.

"Come up when you're ready, Enzo," Dad said.

Then he and Evan headed off to our rooms. To pack.

We had stayed in a different hotel every night on the trip—big, fancy ones, the kind rich and famous people stay in. All of them had huge lobbies and lots of elevators and swimming pools and weight rooms and vending machines . . . and restaurants. I got to order whatever I wanted. I ordered pizza till I got sick of it, then switched to burgers and fries till I got sick of them, then switched to grilled cheese sandwiches, then went back to pizza. I bet if we stacked up all the pizzas we ate, they would have been as tall as the Tower of Pisa—which was Evan's joke, but so what?

When we didn't eat in our hotel's restaurant, or go out to eat, we ordered room service. Room service has to be one of the greatest things ever invented. Anytime you feel like eating something, you just pick up the phone and press a button and someone answers and you tell them what you want and, almost before you hang up, there's a knock at the door and some hotel person in a uniform has a silver tray with a silver dome on it. When they lift the dome—voilà!— there's your pizza, or whatever. It's like having a food genie. Your wish is their command. And it's all delicious. And you get to eat it in bed. And you don't ever have to do any cleaning up; you just put the dirty dishes out in the hall, and later someone comes by and takes it all away. I'd kill to get room service at home.

And not only did the hotel people wash our dishes, they also changed our sheets, made our beds, and cleaned our bathrooms. They even did our laundry. We never had to do anything, ever, except sleep, eat, and watch TV. It was the life.

But it was all over. The big checkout time.

A girl in an apron came by. "You finished?" she asked, all cheerful.

"Completely," I muttered.

"You don't want to take the rest of that up to your room?" she asked.

She looked to be about the same age as my oldest sister, Desi, who was seventeen. She was probably working at the restaurant during the summer to make a little extra money, maybe saving up for college, but more likely saving up for makeup. She was wearing a ton of it.

Girls. I don't get them.

"No, thanks," I said.

She kept clearing, every now and then peeking at me and flashing this big, silly smile. Finally, she said, "Awesome cap."

I reached up and touched the visor of my cap. It was awesome all right. I felt slightly less crushed.

"Thanks," I said.

It all started with the cap. Without the cap, there would have been no trip. No presidency. No stardom. No miracles.

Dad gave it to me the day he told us about the Kap job.

Since I was little, Dad had worked as general manager at G&W Sporting Goods, the dinky chain of mom-and-pop stores that sold boring sporting goods like fishing tackle, golf clubs, and tennis rackets. Then, about a year ago, he decided he had gone as high as he could at G&W and applied to a few different sporting goods places, such as Kap. No one in the family, including Mom, believed he'd even get an interview. People from normal families like ours just didn't get upper management jobs at the coolest athletic and fitness apparel company in the world.

Then Kap called him in for an interview. We were all excited, but we figured that the interview was as far as Dad would get. We didn't tell him that, of course. We wished him luck.

After the interview, Dad told us how the

offices were brand-new and huge and made of steel and glass, and had a fitness center, a game room, and a coffeehouse. He said the employees were all young and hip. Dad was not young or hip. He didn't stand a chance.

But about a month and a half ago—two days before the trip, that is—he came home from work and gathered us in the kitchen for an announcement. My sister Nadine wasn't home, but the rest of us were. And my best friend, Kai, was hanging out at my house that day, so he was there, too.

"I got the Kap job," Dad said, like it wasn't earth-shattering news.

All of us gasped at the same time. Except Mom. She just nodded like a giant bobblehead. She must have already known about it.

I was blinking like crazy, I remember, trying to wake myself up. Finally, I said, "No . . . *way!*"

"Way!" Mom said, and started hopping up and down and clapping.

I couldn't believe it. My old, unhip dad got the superstar dream job! It was our family's first-ever miracle.

We all exploded in total happiness, jumping around and yelling and cheering and high-fiving. Kai, too. Then Mom got out some fancy glasses and a bottle. She popped the cork and filled the glasses with something gold and bubbly. She handed us each one. Kai, too.

He was all, "Whoa! We get to drink *champagne*?"

Mom laughed. "It's just sparkling apple juice, Kai."

"Oh," he said. "I should have known."

We all clinked our glasses together and started chanting, "Kap! Kap! Kap! Kap!" We didn't plan it or anything. We all just did it at the same time. It was like . . . I don't know . . . *magic*. It made us crack up, and that made us slosh our sparkling apple juice, which made us crack up even more. Despite my sisters' giggling and shrieking, and acting dorky in the annoying way they do, I'd say it was probably the best time I'd ever had with my family.

It's not easy having a good time with your family when you have four sisters. That's right: *four* sisters. Desi, Susana, Lupe, and Nadine. I call them the Sisterhood. All of them are teenagers. I'd appreciate some sympathy.

Dad clinked his glass with his wedding ring for quiet. We got quiet pretty darn fast. His first announcement had been amazing, and my hopes were high for the second.

"As part of my training as Kap western states assistant general manager," he said (we applauded), "I will be hitting the open road, traveling the entire length of this great state of California, then venturing into Oregon, Washington, Utah, and Nevada before returning home."

"That sounds like a long trip, Daddy," Lupe, the youngest and annoyingest of my sisters, said. "How long will you be gone?"

Dad looked at Mom, who sighed. They had obviously discussed this before, too.

"The rest of the summer," Dad finally said.

The Sisterhood (minus Nadine, who wasn't home) let out a whiny, *"What?"*

"When do you leave, Daddy?" Lupe asked, on the verge of tears. Lupe is the family drama queen.

"Early tomorrow morning," Dad said, wincing.

The Sisterhood (minus Nadine) wailed.

Me? I was too shocked to make a sound. Dad was going away for the rest of the summer? It was only the middle of July. He was leaving me in the house for a month and a half with five females? This was the worst tragedy in my history. (Up till then.)

Talk about an emotional roller coaster.

"On the plus side," Dad said over the girls' moaning and groaning, "I'll be dropping into Kap outlets, meeting other Kap people, learning the ropes, and checking out the new products, even trying some of them out . . ."

That stopped their sobbing. All of us are real fitness freaks (except Nadine, though she did a few exercisey things like tae kwon do and, for some reason, archery—and, besides, she wasn't there). We got what Dad was saying. He was going to be one of the first people in America to wear and use brand-new, brand-name Kap products, before they hit stores, even, *and* he was going to get paid to wear and use them. We were speechless. Our dad had become a god.

"Do you get to k-keep them?" Susana asked in a hushed voice.

"He does," answered Mom, beaming.

Mom is a personal trainer with her own fitness center in the backyard, and a huge fan of new athletic gear and apparel. Especially apparel. She owns enough clothes to dress every mom in northern California.

Dad smiled like a king. "Fear not, my fine, physically fit family. There will be plenty of Kap perks for everybody from now on."

"Whoa!" Kai breathed.

We all stared off into space, imagining it.

Desi was probably figuring she would become the most popular girl at Pasadero High. She was already popular. She was junior class president last year, in fact. Her dad working for Kap and bringing home lots of cool new clothes would probably make her a lock for student body president next year, her dream. (Why would anyone want to be president? Presidents sit in boring meetings all the time.)

Susana—who is a year younger than Desi, and also athletic, pretty, and smart—didn't care as much about being liked or popular or elected as Desi did. Susana mostly cared about gymnastics. Dad's new job would mean new leotards and maybe some gymnastics equipment at home. Maybe a balance beam, or some crash mats.

Lupe was a cheerleader, and acted like it. I don't mean to stereotype. It's just that she's all the things you probably think of when you think *cheerleader*: stuck-up, sassy, fake, obsessed with her clothes and hair. She seriously believed she was the prettiest, smartest, nicest (ha!), and most talented student at Stanislaus Middle School. I'm sure she expected to top herself in eighth grade—maybe become the prettiest, smartest, nicest, and most talented middle-school student in California, or maybe America, or the *world*. Dad's news probably just made her surer of it.

As far as I knew, Kap didn't make archery equipment or tae kwon do apparel (the little outfits and the colored belts), but Nadine (who wasn't there) wouldn't care. I doubted she would get very excited about Dad's news at all. Nadine doesn't really do excited. Mostly, she slouches, sulks, and writes in her journal.

I realized I was so busy thinking about everybody else's dreams that I didn't have time to come up with anything for myself, and, before I could, Dad pulled out a cap from somewhere.

"This is for you," he said. "It's a prototype. No one in the world has one like it."

The cap was made of blue, stretch-fit material, which meant there wasn't one of those clunky adjustable straps in the back, which was good. The visor was blue, too, and was sturdy and flat, as all great visors should be. The Kap logo—a fat capital *K*—was sewn onto the front of the cap. A smaller one was sewn onto the back.

I glanced at Kai. His mouth was open, but nothing came out. He was overcome by the cap's supreme amazingness.

"Go ahead, Enz," Dad said. "Try it on."

I set the cap on my head and pulled the visor down to eyebrow level, where visors belong. The thing fit like a glove. Dad guided me to the mirror over the couch. I looked like a prince who had just been crowned, but not one of those fancy, old-fashioned princes in tights. More like the Prince of Sports. Like an Olympic gold-medal winner up on a pedestal. I wanted to bow, or do something ceremonial anyway. I stood up straighter, held my shoulders back and my chin up. I curled my lip, made my game face. *Man,* I looked good.

The Sisterhood (minus Nadine), of course, cracked up.

2. The Most Amazingest Trip in the History of Time

The cap revealed its magic later that night, when me and Kai were up in my room.

"Lucky!" "Lucky!" "Lucky!" Kai must have said it a hundred times. That and, "Do you think your dad could get me one?"

He was jealous of the cap. Who wouldn't be? I felt bad for him. Not bad enough to give up the cap, but bad.

"You heard him," I said. "It's a prototype. One of a kind."

"You sure there aren't *two* of a kind?"

"I can't believe Dad got that job," I said, shaking my head.

"That's what I mean. You are so *lucky*. He's probably going to bring home prototypes every day!"

I liked thinking about that.

"It's not so lucky my dad's leaving for a month and a half, though," I said. "He's leaving me alone with *five* girls."

Kai nodded like he understood, but he only had one sister. And a brother. And both of them were younger. Talk about lucky.

"But just think about all the cool stuff he'll bring back," he said, his eyes widening like a pile of treasure had suddenly materialized in front of him.

"Yeah," I said. "I am. But the girls will try to take over while he's gone. I'll be outnumbered."

"You'll just have to pump up the testosterone level. You know. Burp a lot. Be a slob. Say gross things. You'll be all right."

"Don't you remember when my dad was gone for a weekend once and my sisters tried to curl my hair? And *dye* it? I barely escaped."

"I remember. That was a close call." He patted my shoulder. "Tell you what, I'll come over as much as I can. We can race around the house with muddy shoes. Stuff like that. We can beat this thing!"

I wasn't so sure, but said, "Thanks."

Kai was a pretty good guy, despite how puny he was. He was eleven like me, but he sure didn't look it. He looked more like nine. Maybe even eight. It was like he'd stopped growing. I swear he still had baby teeth in front. And his eyes looked way too big for his head. And he wasn't filling out. He was real bony and stumbled around like a newborn horse, his legs going all different directions. He tripped a lot.

It wasn't such a big deal back when we were the same size. We were just two goofy guys running around, acting like crazed monkeys. But I grew taller in fifth grade and filled in some. And I matured. I got more serious. Less goofy. Now I was more like his older brother.

"It sure is an amazing cap," he said, all dazzled again.

"Yeah. I swear there's something . . . I don't know . . . *magical* about—"

Someone knocked on my door right then.

"What?" I barked. I didn't like being interrupted in what I considered to be my private personal space. Plus it was probably just one of my sisters all prepared to annoy me. As usual.

"Can I come in, buddy?"

It was Dad.

"Yeah, sorry," I said in a nicer voice. "Come in."

He stepped inside, kind of awkwardly. He could be a little shy sometimes. Not all dads are bold and brave, I guess. Mine was shy and cautious.

I assumed he was coming in to say he was sorry for abandoning me.

"I just got off the phone," he said, sitting beside me on the bed. "It was Evan Stevens, from work. He's my new supervisor at Kap. He'll be training me and traveling with me."

"Evan Stevens?" Kai asked.

Dad chuckled. "Yep. Like 'even Steven.'"

Kai chuckled, too. I didn't get the joke and didn't care. I wanted to hear what Dad and this Evan guy had talked about. Dad was giving off some seriously strange vibes. He had news and was itching to spill it, but he was taking his time.

"So I was talking to Evan," Dad went on, "telling

him about how excited the family was that I got the job and everything, and he was real glad to hear it. . . . You'll meet him, Enzo. He's a real nice kid. Well, not a *kid*. He's in his twenties. To me he's a kid . . ."

"Yeah," I said, humoring him, wanting him to get to the point. "And . . . ?"

"I told Evan how much you loved the cap, and he said that gave him an idea."

Dad paused a second, then smiled. It was a big, warm, I-have-good-news-for-you smile. Why was he torturing me?

"Tell me his idea, Dad!" I said.

"Well, Evan said maybe having an eleven-year-old boy along on the trip would be a real asset. Maybe an eleven-year-old boy could test out the new products and tell us which ones are amazing and which aren't."

You could have heard a pin drop, even on the carpet.

Then Kai said, "Hey! *Enzo* is an eleven-year-old boy!"

I elbowed him. "So are you, stupid."

"Oh, yeah . . ."

It was totally understandable that he forgot sometimes.

"So?" Dad asked.

"So what?" I asked.

"So do you want to come on the trip with us?"

How do you think I answered?

"Yeah!" Then I gave Dad a shove. He shoved me back, and then we cracked up.

This all happened because of the cap. Dad told Evan Stevens how much I loved it. Evan invited me on the trip. It was the cap. It definitely had some sort of power. Some kind of magic. Luck, maybe. I understood right then I would be lucky as long as I held on to it.

"Lucky," Kai said. He wasn't laughing. He wasn't happy.

I patted him on the shoulder and said, "I'll be back before you know it."

Boy, was I right about that.

The trip started two days later. Me and Dad got up early, way before Mom and the Sisterhood. We had said our good-byes the night before.

After we ate some cereal and did our own dishes (we wouldn't be doing that for a while!) I went out back to say good-bye to our dog, Inkspill, who I call Ink. He's black, of course, although I guess he could also be blue. Come to think of it, he could be purple. Doesn't ink come in just about any color? Well, our Ink was a miniature pinscher—a min pin—and black.

He heard me coming and started yapping and racing around the backyard like a lunatic. I loved Ink and hated leaving him behind. Especially with the Sisterhood. Who knew what they would do to him. A month and a half of baby talk alone would probably damage his brain permanently.

I unlocked the gate, but before I could open it, Ink started hurling himself against it. As usual. He barked and snarled like he was rabid. I couldn't get in.

Then again, I thought to myself, *maybe some time away from him might be a good thing.*

I crouched down and let him lick my face through the chain link.

"Bye, Ink, you big spaz," I said, but in a loving way.

When I returned to the front yard, a car was pulling into the driveway and Dad was walking over to it. It was Evan Stevens come to pick us up. What kind of car did Kap give Evan to drive? Something boxy and boring with good gas mileage? Nope. He drove a silver convertible. With the top down, of course. There was a huge, tilted, black *K* painted on the door. *This* was the car we'd be driving all over the western states! I don't know what one feels like, but it felt like I was having a heart attack. I was that excited.

(Turns out it wasn't a heart attack. Phew. I would've hated to miss the trip.)

Evan shut off the engine, rocked back in his seat, then, with a really big grin, asked, "So what do you think of our ride, boys? Not bad, right?"

Dad laughed and nodded, and I said, "It's awesome!" I admit this was a pretty lame answer, but in this case, it was accurate. I was definitely feeling some awe. Lots of it, actually.

Evan was too cool to live. He was tall, dark, and ripped. His black Kap polo shirt could barely hold his arms, chest, and shoulders. He wore dark Ray-Bans and chewed gum. He smiled real big, but it wasn't fake. He looked wide awake for so early in the morning, like he had more energy than he knew what to do with. He wasn't a spaz like Ink or anything. He just looked . . . you know . . . psyched. Unlike most grown-ups.

I liked him right off the bat.

"How's it going this a.m., Mr. Assistant General Manager?" Evan asked as he shook Dad's hand.

Standing next to Evan, my big, strong father suddenly seemed not so big or strong. But, to be fair, Evan was a lot younger. Dad was ancient. Thirty-eight.

"This has got to be Lorenzo," Evan said, releasing Dad's hand and grabbing mine with a firm grip. "Heard a lot about you, dude. All good."

"H-Hi, Mr. Stevens," I squeaked. I guess I was kind of star-struck.

"Evan is the name," he said. "Mr. Stevens is my granddad's name!"

"I like Enzo," I said, and it struck me that both our names started with *E*. Which was cool.

"So then, Enzo," Evan said, getting real serious all of a sudden, "what do you think about this little excursion we're embarking on?"

I was tongue-tied. What did I *think*? Was I supposed to be thinking? Wasn't this summer vacation? I searched my brain for a thought.

"I think it's going to be the amazingest trip in the history of time," I said.

Evan laughed so hard I bit my tongue. It wasn't that funny. In fact, it wasn't funny at all. *Amazingest* was just a word that had been going around the neighborhood that summer.

"You got that right!" he said. "That's exactly what it's going to be. The amazingest trip in the history of time! You nailed it, Enzo!"

We stowed our gear and piled in, then Evan fired up the convertible and we pulled away from the curb. I leaned back into the seat, which was really cushy and comfortable. I looked up at the blue sky. It was like I was in some PG-13 movie!

We turned the corner onto Kearny Boulevard, a fast street with four lanes of traffic. As the car picked up speed, the wind got under the visor of my cap and started to lift it. My hands went up like lightning and grabbed it tight. Nothing was ever going to separate me from my magic.

Or so I believed . . .

I thought about keeping a journal so I wouldn't forget any of the amazing things that we were going to do, but that felt too schoolish, so instead I texted the info to Kai. Kai saved all my messages and showed them to me when I got back. Here's some of the amazingest ones, in the order I sent them:

frisco! cable car! alcatraz!!!

HOTEL!! room service! day n nite!!!

boogie boarded in pac ocean! B-) . . . saw WHALE!!!
   i think . . .

hiked big sur in cool nu kap boots!!!

snorkeld in montarey!!!

cable video games in room . . . wieght room . . . pool.

crash on hwy! fire! scary!!! :-o

saw U2!!! old guys but amazing!! almost met bono!!!

parasurfing!!!!!!!!!!

met lebron james!!!! he signed my kap cap!!

130 in deth vally! all hail a/c!!!

ginormus water park!!! :-D

hollywood!! studio tour got u suvineer

guess who got jack blacks autograf?!! hes really fat

hollywood kap store . . . indoor rappids!!!

1 word . . . disneyland!!!

water skiing on lake tahoe!!!

snow skiing in teh summer!!!

camped on beach . . . elk! ur not sposed to look em

   in the eye . . . i didn't . . . evan did . . . brave dude!! . . .

   nuthin happend :-(

hiked in rain forest! it didnt rain :-\

seattle . . . space needle! mariners game!

DEFINITLY saw a whale this time!!!! dad sawit to

did u know the eifel tower was in vegas? it is!!! :-o

hoover DAM!! really big DAM!! DAM!! ;-)

touch football w/ dad evan n kap guys!!!

hanglided!!! wo!!! wish u were here!!!

I didn't really mean that last bit, but I didn't
want him to know I was glad he wasn't with
us. It was nice to have someone at home to tell
about all the cool things I was doing, someone

who would be totally jealous. Kai was perfect for that.

Dad and I got to hang out together a lot, which we never got to do at home, because he was always working or helping the Sisterhood with their many, many issues. As it turns out, he's a good guy to hang with. He wasn't so fussy about stuff, like Mom is. He didn't bother me about baths or changing my clothes or picking up my things. He never said I should avoid junk food or fried food or fast food or carbs. He never checked fat or sugar content on labels. He never nagged me about watching too much TV or playing video games too much. He was kind of cool.

We bonded, as they say, but in a real guy way, a way he and the Sisterhood could never bond, because they weren't guys, like we were. This might sound totally cheesy, but of all the amazing things we did on the trip, getting so much one-on-one time with my dad was probably the best.

I was right. That did sound cheesy.

"Dad, this is the best time I've ever had with you," I blurted out once when we were standing in line for a roller coaster. "Then again, it's the best time I've ever *had*."

"I'm having a ball, too, Enz," he answered. "Let's enjoy it while it lasts. It'll be over before you know it."

Before I knew it, it was over.

3. Big Changes

After we checked out of the hotel in Sacramento, Evan and Dad had one more call to make, in Stockton, before we headed home. I stayed in the car. I wasn't pouting. Pouting is a tactic for getting your parents to do what you want them to do, and there was nothing my dad or mom could do this time. Parents may have all the power in a family, but even they are powerless when it comes to school. School tells parents what to do.

I didn't stay in the car to pout. I was mourning the loss of the most amazingest summer vacation in the history of summer vacations. I was grieving the death of total, supreme, nonstop fun.

Evan and Dad didn't pout or mourn. That's because their joyride wasn't over. They would get to keep driving around in a silver convertible, trying out cool new sporting goods and sports-wear, meeting famous athletes and entertainers, staying in hotels, ordering room service, and bouncing on beds. Okay, maybe not bouncing on beds. But they would get to keep on joyriding, *and* getting paid for it, while I died of boredom in school.

The first time I glanced out from under my visor, we were on Kearny Boulevard—back in Pasadero already. Then we turned again and, just like that, we were home.

Mom, Desi, Susana, and Lupe rushed from the house when we pulled up. They swarmed Dad, squealing and chattering and hugging and kissing him, and, of course, asking what he'd brought home for them.

Nadine brought up the rear. She was dressed like some girl from the olden days going to a tea party: frilly wide-brimmed hat, poufy dress to the ground, ruffly collar and sleeves, black lace-up boots. The only difference was that she was wearing white makeup on her face and black lipstick. Apparently, this was her new look: Goth-slash–American Girl. She liked to change it now and then. Not sure why she chose heavy clothes and makeup in August. In California.

When she caught up, she said, "Hello, Father," mostly to the ground. Dad hugged her and knocked her big, floppy hat off.

Mom was the only one to take any notice of me, which was fine until she started smooching me all over and talking baby talk. That's when my face got all hot and my vision got all blurry and I realized I was going to cry. No way was I going to cry in front of Evan.

I wriggled free and snapped, "Stop it! I can't breathe!"

She laughed. "So you're too big now to be hugged and kissed by your mama, Lenchito?"

Lenchito was my mom's Spanish nickname for me. Only she got to call me that. Sometimes one of my sisters would slip and I was forced to headlock her till she swore she'd never say it again, or till Mom or Dad broke it up.

"Yes," I answered, but she jumped into the backseat anyway and went totally nuts with the stupid hugs and kisses and mushy talk stuff. I fought her off for a while, which was kind of fun, and which stopped the tears from falling, thank goodness. We rolled around in the backseat, wrestling and tickling each other, till suddenly I screeched: "My *cap*! You'll bend the visor!"

Everyone laughed.

I reached up to check my cap, and . . .

"Where is it?" I shrieked.

More laughter.

"MOM! Where is it? Are you *sitting* on it?"

Oh, the horror I felt in those few seconds. Even reliving it now makes my heart thump in my throat.

"I got it," Evan said from the driver's seat, and held it up. "Figured I'd better get it out of harm's way. Or, in this case, *Mom's* way."

I could have kissed him. Not really, but I was really glad he was there and knew what to do. He was a man of good instincts and priorities.

I took the cap from him, put it on, then checked my look in the rearview mirror.

Mom and the Sisterhood (minus Nadine) cracked up.

"What?" I asked.

"Someone got *conceited*," Lupe taunted, and

everyone (except Nadine) cracked up again.

"What are you talking about?"

"And no wonder," Mom said, looking me up and down. "Just look at you!"

"What?" I asked again, trying to look at myself. (Why do people say that? It can't be done.) "What's wrong with me?"

Everyone was looking at me—except Nadine, who had taken out her black journal and was writing in it.

"There's nothing wrong," Mom said. "You're just so . . ."

"Buff?" Evan piped in.

The Sisterhood (minus Nadine) giggled.

"Exactly!" Desi said.

"And tan," Susana chipped in.

My sisters (minus Nadine) were looking at me. *Really* looking at me. And grinning. This made me extremely uncomfortable.

Mom said, "It's amazing what a summer vacation can do to a kid."

What was all this? If I'd changed, why hadn't Dad or Evan said anything about it? Maybe because guys don't usually sit around talking about how each other looks. Plus we'd been together practically every second, and it's hard to see people change when you're with them all the time. It's hard to see yourself change, too. It happens slowly, like grass growing. When I looked at myself in the mirror or in pictures, all I saw was my cap and my amazing new clothes.

Mom and the girls hadn't seen me in a month and a half. A month and a half of fun and sun. I bet I had changed. I wondered how.

I jumped out of the car and bolted for the house.

I heard Ink yapping and scratching from the other side of the front door as I approached it. When I pushed it open, he freaked out all over me, jumping and pawing and slobbering and whining. I was glad to see him, but I was on a mission.

"Down, Ink! Sit! *Sit!*" I commanded.

He didn't obey. Big shock.

I tore off through the house with him hot on my heels. Nipping at them, actually. I shut the bathroom door on him, then turned to face the full-length mirror. A very tanned Enzo Harpold, wearing a new black T-shirt with a metallic silver Kap logo on the front, untucked, looked back at me. He was wearing a most excellent pair of Kap athletic shoes, white with a blue logo, unlaced, and new baggy plaid Kap shorts. The guy was sharply dressed, that's for sure. But what about this buff stuff?

My shirt did hang different: tighter in the shoulders, looser around my stomach. My shoulders looked different, too, somehow. Broader, I guess. I bent my arms and clenched my fists. *Hey.* There was definition in those biceps. And in my calf muscles, my forearms, even in my neck. I sucked in my stomach and puffed out my chest and—*whoa!*—I had a chest! One that was actually wider than my stomach, I mean. I turned sideways. My stomach was less pudgy than it used to be. I lifted my T-shirt and did an ab crunch. Not bad! Not exactly washboard, but sort of ripply.

Now, it's not like I was a total loser before the trip. I had been built pretty average and was happy that way. Me and Kai had never cared about that stuff. We never looked in mirrors. We didn't bathe unless we had to. We wore the same clothes for as long as we could get away with it. We were guys. We hung out. We had fun. Who cared what we looked like?

But now I was looking in the mirror. I was staring in it. I had changed. Big time. Mom and the Sisterhood (minus Nadine) were right: I was buff.

The cap, I thought. *The cap did this.*

I reached up and pulled it off. My hair piled out. It had gotten pretty long. Down to my eyebrows and earlobes. I hadn't gotten a haircut on the trip. And it was lighter from the sun.

Uh-oh, I thought with dread. *Am I cute?*

4. Little Changes

When I stepped out of the bathroom, Ink was still there, practically dying for attention. So I gave him some and noticed right off he had changed, too.

"Who pierced Ink's ears?" I screamed.

I ran back outside and confronted the Sisterhood, who were still gathered by Evan's car. Except Nadine, who was sitting on the lawn, writing in her journal.

"Who did it?" I yelled. "Who pierced my dog's ears?"

Evan laughed.

"Nobody did," Lupe said.

"Well, he's wearing earrings," I said, pointing at them.

"Those are studs," Lupe said.

"Are you crazy? You pierced a *dog's* ears? Isn't that illegal? Cruelty to animals or something?"

"We didn't pierce Inky's ears, Enzo," Mom said. "They're magnetic."

"Oh," I said, and calmed down a little. I was relieved they had the good sense not to stick some big needle through my poor dog's ears.

"Magnetic?" I asked. "Magnetic dog earrings?"

"Studs," Lupe said. "Rings could be dangerous. Inky could hook a claw in them when he scratched—"

"But wait a minute," I said, feeling upset again. "I don't want earrings in my dog's ears!"

"Studs," Lupe said.

She was really asking for it.

"Take them out," I said to everyone listening.

No one moved.

"Then I'll do it," I said, and rushed at Ink.

Lupe stepped between us.

"He's not just *your* dog, Enzo," she said, crossing her arms in front of her like she was the queen of me.

I looked around at the others.

"We all like them," Desi said.

Susana nodded.

I turned to Dad. I knew I could count on him, at least.

He shrugged. The coward.

I tried Nadine. She was against so many things for so many reasons that I couldn't imagine her standing by and letting people put earrings on a dog, especially without the dog's permission. Nadine's all about rights.

"What about you?" I asked. "You can't like this."

She didn't look up from her journal. She was staying out of it.

"We thought it was a fun idea, Enzo," Mom said. "They don't hurt him, you know."

"I knew you'd do this," I said to all of them. "I knew you'd try to turn my dog into a girl while I was gone."

Everybody laughed.

"I mean it," I said. "Don't you think there are enough girls in this family already?" I was really hopping mad. I was actually hopping.

"Calm down, Enz," Dad said.

"Calm down? Look what they did to him,

Dad! My dog's wearing *diamond studs*!"

"Pirates wore earrings," Evan said.

I idolized the guy, but I sure wished right then he would butt out.

"You're crazy!" I yelled. "All of you! Take those earrings out of my dog *right now*!"

"You can't make decisions for everybody," Desi said. "We'd have to put it to a vote."

Desi loved to vote on things. Who's prettiest in her grade at school, for example. Or most popular.

"Can I tell you what you can do with your vote?" I said.

"Okay, okay, that's enough," Mom said. "We can talk about this later. Right now, let's say adios to Evan and get our guys settled back in. I'm sure there will be a lot of new things for them to get used to. . . ."

"What new things?" Dad asked.

"Just some little changes, honey," Mom said, putting her arm around him.

"What changes?" I asked.

"Tranquilo," Mom said.

I seethed. This is what she always says when

someone starts getting mad at her. It means calm down, and it usually makes people madder.

"What changes?" I demanded.

"I really should be on my way," Evan said.

"Thank you for taking such good care of my men," Mom said. "And I hope you'll come to our Labor Day *asado* tomorrow. Bring a date if you like."

An *asado* is an Argentinean barbecue. My mom was born in Argentina. Her family lives there. I hoped Evan would come, but without a girl. We had plenty of those.

"I'm girlfriendless at the moment, Tina," Evan said. "A rolling stone gathers no *miss*."

Mom and Dad laughed, so it must have been a joke. Evan was always saying things that made adults laugh. I looked forward to the day when I could do that. When you can tell jokes over kids' heads, you know you're a man.

I was relieved he'd be coming back the next day, so we wouldn't have to have a big, gooey good-bye scene. I hated big, gooey good-bye scenes.

Evan gave me an air five, then left. Perfect.

"Let's get you two inside," Mom said. "We want to hear all about the trip. And we can't wait to see what you think of our little changes."

Nadine coughed.

"Except Nadine, that is," Lupe said. "She wants you both to know she had no part in what we did."

Nadine nodded and closed her journal.

I had already been in the house, but I had been in such a mad rush to look at my buffness I hadn't noticed anything around me. This time, though, I braced myself for what Mom and the Sisterhood (minus Nadine) had done to it.

The first thing to hit me was the stink. It smelled like a hundred grandmas having a quilting bee. I couldn't breathe. I was dying. I'm serious.

"Can we open a window?" Dad asked.

"Can we open all the windows?" I gasped.

Dad and I started unlocking and opening windows. A lot of them were pretty stuck. Had they been locked the whole time we were gone? Probably. Females are always cold.

"Was there a fire sale at the candle shop?" Dad asked.

He was right. There were candles everywhere: on tables, windowsills, the mantel, even the floor.

Mom laughed. "Oh, you're funny!" She was flirting with him. That's another way she keeps him from getting mad at her. It's gross.

"And new furniture," Dad said, "and new paint. These are 'little changes,' Tina?"

"Uh, Daddy, our old couch was a hundred years old," Lupe said.

"We did the painting ourselves," said Susana. "To save money."

"You should check out your room," Lupe said to me. Sinisterly.

"*Sí*, Lenchito!" Mom said, clapping her hands together. "I can't wait to see what you think!"

"Me either," Lupe said.

"What did you do to my room?" I asked, terrified.

Mom laughed again.

Lupe didn't. But she sure smiled.

I ran upstairs. There were more changes along

the way, but I didn't stop to take them in. I rushed like a guy whose home was hit by a hurricane while he was on vacation. Which was sort of what I was.

I froze when I came to the door to my room. It was shut. The NO GIRLS *ALOUD* sign was gone. So was the foil mirror I bought at the mall with the words IF YOU SEE A GIRL, GET LOST! printed at the bottom. The door was bare and had been painted turquoise. I couldn't remember what color it had been before, but I was sure it wasn't turquoise.

I stood staring in horror at the door so long that Mom, Dad, and the Sisterhood (minus Nadine) caught up to me.

"Well?" Mom asked. "Aren't you going to open it?"

She reached past me, turned the new glass doorknob, pushed the door open, and there it was: the room formerly known as Enzo's. Everything was gone. Everything. There was nothing on the walls. Nothing on my dresser or my bed or my desk or my floor. Nothing. It was a nightmare come true.

"W-Where's all my stuff?" I finally managed to say.

"In your closet, in boxes," Mom said. "We took great care in taking it down. We knew you'd want to do the arranging."

I looked at her. She smiled at me, totally unaware that I was on the verge of strangling her.

"Great care?" I asked, trying to contain my rage. I couldn't.

"ARE YOU *KIDDING* ME!" I yelled.

"Tranquilo," Mom cooed.

Before I could go psycho on her, Dad gripped my shoulders, leaned in close, and whispered in my ear, "All good things must come to an end."

"But *Dad*!" I squawked. No way could he cave to this!

He gripped my shoulders tighter. "*Their* good thing," he said into my ear so that only I could hear him. "*Their* good thing is coming to an end. We're *back*."

"Ohhh," I breathed, getting his meaning.

It was take-back time.

"You at least like the *color*, don't you?" Susana asked, as if offended. "I hope so. It took us for*ever* to get the right shades."

I looked at the walls. Two were blue. Two were

gray. They alternated. The ceiling was gray. I had to admit I kind of liked it.

"Let's leave Enzo alone," Mom said, ushering the girls out. "He needs time to get used to the changes."

She left, too. Only me and Dad remained. I sat down on my bed. It had a new spread: dark brown with a blue border. I kind of liked it, too.

Dad sat next to me.

"'Little changes,'" he said, and raised his eyebrows.

"Yeah," I said, nodding.

But they weren't all bad.

5. Stan

I got one day between coming home from the Kap trip and returning to school, one day to shift from Drive to Neutral to Park. I shifted so fast, I think I blew my transmission.

At least that's how I felt the morning after Labor Day, after the barbecue, on my first day of middle school. I couldn't get into gear. I hadn't gotten to sleep the night before till well after midnight. I was still in the habit of staying up late. I was still in the habit of having fun. Plus I was kind of jittery about going to Stan for the first time.

Stanislaus Middle School was its real name, but everyone called it Stan. All four Pasadero elementary schools emptied into it after fifth grade. That meant there were going to be a lot of kids I didn't know, a new enormous building to get lost in, a new principal, new teachers, new everything. And I wouldn't be staying in one classroom anymore. I'd have a new room, a new teacher, and a new subject every fifty-five minutes. With all this to look forward to, it's no wonder I had trouble getting to sleep that night. And trouble waking up the next morning.

Mom opened my curtains at seven and told me to get up. I rolled over and fell back asleep. She came back again and again, bouncing my mattress, pinching my nose, pulling off my blankets, threatening to pour a glass of cold water on me. I didn't so much as open my eyes.

It took her and Dad together to drag me out of bed and downstairs. They dropped me into a chair at the kitchen table. I dropped my head on the table and fell asleep.

"He's tired," Mom said brilliantly.

"He's faking," Dad said more brilliantly.

Mom put food in front of me: cheesy scrambled eggs and toast and melon.

"Coffee," I groaned.

Mom laughed. "How about orange juice?"

I pounded the table with my fist. "Coffee!"

"Did you let him have coffee on the trip?" Mom asked Dad.

"Sometimes . . . a little decaf . . . ," Dad said. The rat.

Mom poured some decaf into a mug and set it down beside me. I stirred in my usual six spoonfuls of sugar and some half-and-half to cool it off, and gulped it down.

I banged the table, making my mug dance, and roared, "Coffee!"

They didn't refill my cup. Instead, they hustled me out the door.

As I leaned against the bus stop sign, waiting for the bus, I went over in my mind the advice Evan had given me at the barbecue.

"Wear T-shirts, jeans, and athletic shoes, preferably ones made by Kap."

No problem there, especially about the Kap gear. I was wearing it head to toe.

"Don't wear jewelry. No bling. Nothing a wise guy could grab hold of."

No-brainer. You'd never see bling on me. But then I bet that's what poor Ink had thought . . .

"Take off your cap in the halls, or lose it."

What a horrifying thought!

"Don't carry your schoolbooks in your hands. Stow them in your backpack."

"Duct-tape over any vents in your locker from the inside so that no one can slip things in."

"Don't bother talking to your upper classmen. Avoid them like the plague, especially your first year."

"Keep your priorities straight. Number one: athletics. Number two: athletics. Number three: Kap athletic wear and gear. Number four: never run for elected office. That's for chumps. Number five: athletics."

I was going to follow his advice. I figured if I focused on athletics, I would stay fit (take that, bullies!), stay alert (take that, pranksters!), have some fun at least (take that, parents!), and be able to show off my cool new gear (take that, all you middle schoolers whose dads didn't work at Kap!). Athletics was my game plan for surviving middle school.

Lupe was at the bus stop with me. She had finished sixth and seventh grades and was starting her last year at Stan. She looked wide awake and even eager, and wore a new outfit and plenty of makeup. Her eyelashes were caked with little black clumps. This was her first year of wearing makeup to school.

We didn't stand near each other, of course, or act like we knew each other. Lupe had big plans for eighth grade. She wanted to be Stan's queen, so she wasn't going to risk her reputation by being seen with a lowly sixth-grade boy.

When the bus pulled up, Lupe hopped up and down and waved at girls through the windows. She squealed after she boarded the bus, then raced down the aisle into the arms of her squealing friends. They all hugged and squealed and chattered. Girls are like rodents.

I was still leaning against the no-parking sign. The bus driver asked me if I was coming. She looked pretty frazzled for Day One. I bet bus drivers dread school, too.

I trudged onto the bus. No one mobbed me.

Kai trudged onto the bus a few stops later. No one mobbed him, either. I sat and waited for him to trudge down the aisle and plop down next to me. He wasn't happy about this back-to-school thing, either.

It had been a long time since we'd seen each other, but I didn't want to make a big fuss about it, especially on a school bus. Also, I don't like big, stupid, gooey helloes any more than I like big, stupid, gooey good-byes.

Kai understood. He just said, "Hey, Enz."

"Hey," I answered.

He looked pretty much the same as he did in July, except he was way frecklier. The sun always did that to him. His freckles got bigger and bigger till they fused together into a giant brown blob covering his whole body. He still had his dark, rusty, tangly mop of hair, like Annie's in *Annie*. What middle-school guy wants to look like Annie? Not me.

I realized right then what I needed to do to my cute, long blond hair.

"We should get crew cuts," I said.

He nodded.

"You seem bigger," he said, looking me up and down.

This made me uncomfortable. I didn't like

being checked out by another guy.

"What do you mean, 'bigger'?" I asked.

"Bigger. You know. Kind of . . . buff."

He was right, of course. I was buff. And I kind of liked being buff, but I still didn't like it being pointed out, especially by Kai, who I assumed was feeling jealous. The guy had always been as scrawny as a scarecrow. A short scarecrow. And he dressed like a scarecrow. I think he had on the same shirt and shorts he did the day before me and Dad left on the trip. I wondered if they'd been washed in between.

"I hate the first day of school *so* much," I said.

"Me, too," he said.

"And I hate the second day."

"And the third one," he said, starting to grin.

"All right," I said. "Let's not go through the whole school year."

"Hey, did you really meet LeBron James?"

I took off my cap and showed him where LeBron signed it with a metallic silver marker.

"Can I touch it?" he asked in a whisper of awe and respect.

"Are your hands clean?"

"Huh? Yeah. I guess . . ."

"Kidding," I said, and handed him the cap.

He touched the signature lightly, tracing it with the tip of his finger. Then he held the cap at arm's length to admire it. He kept shaking his head, like he couldn't believe it was real.

"This is the amazingest cap in the history of the whole megaverse." His eyes were kind of wet.

I had to agree. "Yeah, and it was the most amazingest *trip* in the history of the whole megaverse."

"It sure sounded like it in your texts."

"Oh, man, the texts didn't even come close to what it was really like."

He nodded. I think he could tell that something earth-shatteringly major had happened to me. When he looked at me, it was like I wasn't Enzo Harpold anymore. It was more like I was famous. Maybe superhuman.

That made me uncomfortable, too, but in a way I was way more comfortable with.

Stan was a big brick block of a building. It looked like a prison, but then don't all schools?

Aren't all schools?

Kids were pouring out of buses and cars and into Stan's front doors, all of them probably thinking pretty much what I was thinking: *Blah* or *Ugh* or *Burn down the school!*

I'd been to an orientation in the spring, so I knew the basic layout of the place. But that didn't mean I knew where to go. I'd gotten a schedule during the summer in the mail that listed what classes I had, what rooms they were in, and what teachers taught them. I had it in my hand, but in my fog of sleep deprivation, it looked like Chinese.

A dull electronic tone came over the intercom. *MOOOOOP!* What did it mean? Was it a warning bell? Tardy bell? I waited for a voice to explain, the way flight attendants do. *The principal would like all students to return to their seats . . .* Or homerooms, or whatever. I wanted to return to my bed. No one explained anything.

"Should we send up a flare?" Kai asked.

"Got one?"

"We could ask for help?"

You don't start middle school by asking for directions. Everyone knew that. Even I knew that. Kai was so clueless.

"Go ahead," I said, deciding that giving humiliating tasks to inferiors was acceptable middle-school behavior. I mean, I was definitely better looking, better dressed, and, let's face it, hotter than Kai, so why shouldn't I start right off asserting my superiority? Over one person, at least.

"Who should I ask?" Kai asked.

There was probably a New Students Help Center somewhere, but again, I knew by instinct that standing in a line of clueless underclassmen would tattoo me a dork. I remembered Evan's advice about staying away from upperclassmen, but if we didn't ask one of them, we'd have to ask some other lost sixth grader.

"Ask an eighth grader," I suggested, a bit surprised at how easily I was willing to sacrifice my friend to protect my reputation. It was every kid for himself in middle school.

"How can you tell which ones are in eighth grade?" Kai asked.

My opinion of him was sinking fast—though it hadn't been too high for months. Picking out members of the older class did not require special knowledge. The eighth graders were taller, cooler, cockier, and laughing their butts off at the dopey sixth graders standing around in a daze, their schedules drooping in their hands. Like us.

I pointed to a knot of jocks in gray hoodies and baggy pants and said, "Try one of them. They look eager to help."

Kai gulped.

"Go on," I said, shoving him into the lion's den.

He stopped going forward when the shove wore off and peeked back at me.

"Go!" I mouthed.

He made a face like the Cowardly Lion, then tiptoed toward the jocks. When he reached them, he asked his question. I couldn't hear it over the hall noise, but I sure heard the jocks bust out laughing. One of them poked Kai in the chest, then brought his finger up and flicked Kai's nose. More yuks. When Kai turned to leave, the poking jock stuck out his foot and tripped him. Luckily, Kai didn't fall onto his face. He just did some herky-jerky robotic moves trying to keep his balance till he ran into some girl.

I walked away quickly, like I didn't know him. He caught up to me. I walked faster. He cornered me when the traffic jammed.

"Look," I said out of the corner of my mouth, not looking at him. "We have different home-rooms. Let's split up and meet outside at the end of the day."

"What about lunch?" Kai asked.

I glanced back to see if the jocks were still looking at us. I couldn't see them.

"Maybe," I whispered.

The bottleneck cleared and I slipped into the crowd, trying—yeah, I admit it—to ditch him. He kept after me for a while, until at last I was forced to glare at him and whisper, *"Go on!"* Which he got. He turned around and joined the flow of traffic going the way we'd come.

"Congratulations," a voice beside me said.

It was Iris Pok, a girl from my elementary school. We had been in fifth grade together.

Iris loved running guys down, as if it were a sport, or her job. She was one of those girls who thought girls were smarter, more mature, and just all-round *better* than boys—and she was constantly trying to prove this by messing with guys' heads so much they went insane.

"Congratulations?" I asked.

"For dumping your loyal best friend in the first moments of your middle-school career," she said, then did a triple eyelid flutter. (All my sisters—except Nadine—did this when they felt better than me. I think it's supposed to mean, *Can I trust my eyes? Are you really as* [add insult here] *as you seem?*)

"Step off, Iris," I said. "I'm looking for my homeroom."

She snatched the schedule from my hand.

I started to yell "Hey!" but stopped myself. I didn't want people to think some girl could get me all worked up.

"We're in the same homeroom," she said, reading the schedule. "We can walk together."

Though she was a girl, Iris wasn't a total loser. She was athletic, with dark skin and almost black eyes. She was taller than me, though over the summer I'd gained a little ground on her. She wore T-shirts and jeans and athletic shoes, not skirts and tights and dresses like most girls. She didn't wear makeup or jewelry. She ran fast. She was smart. And mean. She sort of scared me.

"That's okay," I said. I thought instead I'd lay back and follow her.

"Right," she said, a look of extreme smugness on her face. "I predict you will go far at Stan."

Then she walked off. Over her shoulder, she added, "Nice cap."

6. Notice

There was nothing homey about homeroom. Or roomy, for that matter. It was packed with kids. Only a few of them had come from Tuolomne, my old school, including Iris, who chose a seat across the aisle from me, probably so I'd be within teasing distance. The teacher, Ms. Boech (rhymes with joke), called roll, then gave us each a handbook of Stan's rules and procedures. A *fat* handbook.

Rule number one: Always have your handbook with you while at school.

Great. We all had to lug around a brick in our backpacks. We'd be hunchbacks in no time.

Number two: Always remove headwear (hats, caps, hoods, etc.) when you enter a classroom.

I grumbled and took off my cap. A few girls

behind me giggled and whispered. *Hat head*, I thought, and loosened my hair with my fingers

One section of the handbook described "consequences," better known as punishments, for breaking the school rules. The lightest sentence was a "think time": fifteen minutes to yourself to "reconsider your choices." Get three think times and you were slapped with a lunch detention. This meant eating your lunch in a classroom with other juvenile delinquents instead of in the cafeteria. After that came an after-school detention, then community service (having to do chores around the school), suspension (not being allowed to come to school for a short period of time), and, finally, expulsion (getting kicked out for good). You couldn't get the Big E unless you had gone through all the other "consequences," unfortunately.

Ms. Boech went on and on and on over-explaining each point in the handbook till I was tempted to put my cap back on and take a think time so I could get out of there. Why were they coming down on us so hard right on the first day? It felt like boot camp. What happened to

"Welcome! We're glad you're here!"? Why was it, "Watch it, kid! Screw up and it will hurt!" I felt younger instead of older, like Stan trusted me less than Tuolomne did, like the older I got, the more they expected me to act out. Why? What were they so afraid of?

Meanwhile, I became aware that the giggling and whispering behind me was spreading. I felt eyes on me. I slyly rubbed my nose, then checked my fingers: nothing. Why were they staring? I saw notes getting passed, which I found pretty brave considering Ms. Boech was up there explaining the tortures we'd receive for acting out in class. What was it about me that was worth getting into trouble for?

And then it hit me. The *cap*! They'd all seen it. Naturally, they were all impressed and felt the need to spread the word.

One thing we had to do during that first homeroom was nominate officers for the year: president, vice president, treasurer, and secretary. That didn't make any sense to me. We were mostly strangers to each other. Shouldn't we get to know each other awhile before electing our leaders? Iris raised her hand and asked that exact question, and Ms. Boech explained we had to do it now so that the officers could get to work right away.

"There will be a general election first," she told us. "The top five vote getters will then make a speech, after which there will be a run-off vote. You may nominate any sixth grader you know. You may not, however, nominate yourself."

I worried Kai might be at that very moment nominating me over in his homeroom, then figured it couldn't possibly make a difference. How could I win before anybody knew me? I guessed that the people who'd had the most friends in their old school would be elected. I had not been popular in my old school. So I blew a sigh of relief.

A few kids nominated other kids and Ms. Boech wrote the names down. Then this girl behind me said, "I nominate him. The boy with the Kap cap on his desk."

I turned around to find she was pointing at me.

"Me?" I croaked.

Some kids laughed. A few girls blushed and giggled.

"You have to know his name," Ms. Boech told the girl.

Whew!

"His name is Enzo. Enzo Harpold," Iris said.

I glared at her.

"I nominate Enzo Harpold," the girl said.

"I second the motion," chimed Iris.

I started to object, to tell Ms. Boech I didn't want to be president, and not to write my name on the list, but all around me people were whispering my name. I hadn't forgotten what Evan said about never running for elected office. I was just suddenly curious to see how many votes I'd get. I'd already gotten one vote from someone I didn't even know. I had a feeling some of the people staring at me and whispering might vote for me, too.

My oldest sister, Desi, was the one who was supposed to care so much about votes. Lupe, too. Not me. But I did like the idea of a sudden rise to fame and power—on the first day at a new school! And being president, being in charge, could sure make going to middle school a lot easier.

So I defied Evan's advice and kept my mouth shut.

My next class was P.E. Stan's gym was a stadium compared to Tuolomne's, and I'd seen plenty of stadiums that summer. The teacher, Mr. Keller, acted pretty tough and strict, saying he would not tolerate any shenanigans. That's one of those words only adults use, but I knew what it meant. He distributed gray gym shorts and T-shirts with the Stan mascot on it, a snarling cartoon badger, then assigned lockers.

In elementary school we didn't have to change clothes for P.E. We weren't in elementary school anymore. I felt some eyes on me as I undressed, and figured it was because of the clothes, the shoes, and, of course, the cap. It was all Kap, and it was all brand-new—not just to me, but to anybody. My outfitting was cutting edge. I knew that. And then when my clothes were off (not *all* of them, of course), I figured they kept staring because of my buffness. Which made me uncomfortable. I pretended not to notice and quickly pulled on my gym clothes.

I stowed my clothes in my locker, set my cap on the metal shelf overhead, then walked back out to the gym. Two jocks came up to me, the jocks from the hall, the ones who had tormented Kai. They weren't upperclassmen after all. If these two guys had come up to me before the summer, I probably would have worried they were going to torment me, too. But I knew why they were coming over that day in the gym. I had passed some sort of test. They were coming over to invite me into their jock world. Not formally or anything. The coming over was the invitation.

I acted casual, as if it was no big deal.

"What do you think of Killer?" the one who tormented Kai said. He was about my height with dark hair. He had a disgusted look on his face.

"I've had worse," I said.

"Where you from, dude?" the other guy said. He was blond with a kind of squarish face. He was a little shorter than me, but he stood up so straight you barely noticed it. He didn't slouch, like most of us do. He smiled a real smile.

"Pasadero," I said.

"Yeah, but what school?"

"Tuolomne."

"Ohhh," the scowler said, like where I went to elementary school explained something to him.

"I'm Chase," the blond guy with the good posture and smile said. "This is Lance. We went to San Joaquin."

He said this with some pride, and it seemed to puff up Lance a bit, too. I'd heard the kids from San Joaquin thought they were pretty hot.

"Yeah?" I answered, like it meant nothing to me.

They looked at each other. Lance shook his head. In disgust. Chase chuckled.

"You got a name?" he asked me.

"Enzo," I said.

"Enzo?" Lance asked.

"Lorenzo to you," I said.

Chase chuckled again. The guy laughed easy. I liked that.

"Enzo for short, huh?" he asked.

"That's right."

"You Mexican?" Lance asked.

Something told me he wouldn't approve if I was. But I wasn't going to lie.

"My mom's from Argentina," I said.

"Cool," Chase said. "Do you speak Spani—?"

"Where's Argentina?" Lance interrupted.

"It's in Mexico," I said.

Chase laughed again. Lance was getting sore.

"Here comes Killer," Chase said, wiping his smile away with the back of his hand. "Look busy."

We did some stretching and some calisthenics. Then the coach had us run a lap out on the track behind the school, which was a piece of cake. For me, anyway. Some guys looked like they might die halfway around. They probably spent all summer inside, staring at screens.

Like Evan says: Those who do, do; those who don't, watch.

I crossed the finish line first.

"Fine job," Mr. Keller said as I passed him. "Good hustle."

Chase and Lance came in second and third. Lance was seriously sore at me by then.

"You're in good shape," Chase said to me, a bit winded.

I thought about telling him about my trip, but decided to wait. If I spilled it all too fast, it would have made me seem too eager to talk about it, too impressed with myself. I had already impressed them. I decided to leak the story out a little at a time.

Chase was in my next class, math, so we sat together. After that was lunch, so we walked through the crowded halls together. We didn't talk much. We were too busy checking everybody out, and checking everybody checking us out. Chase did mention that he and Lance hung out at the skate park a lot. I'd never gone there before. I'd always been too afraid. Not anymore. *Bring it on!* I thought.

The cafeteria was as big as the gym. We got in the long line for our food. Lance stormed up, his face all red. Sore again. This was one cranky dude.

"Why didn't you wait?" he asked Chase.

Chase shrugged. "Me and Enz had math together, so we walked over. Big deal."

Lance seethed.

A boy wearing a vest and a bow tie standing behind us said, "Hey, no cuts!"

Chase just laughed, but Lance vented his anger at Chase and me on this poor little kid. He got right into the little kid's face, and said, "What are you going to do about it, little piggy—squeal?"

The kid didn't flinch. "My house happens to be made of bricks, Mr. Wolf. You couldn't get in."

Chase busted a gut. "Go ahead, Lance! Huff and puff!"

I stepped up to Lance. "Leave the kid alone. He's right. I hate it when someone cuts in front of me."

This was risky, but not nearly as risky as hang gliding or parasailing. Besides, I had the cap. What could happen?

Chase stopped laughing. Lance glared at me. If looks could kill . . .

"Yeah, back of the line, Mr. Wolf," the kid in the bow tie said. I gave him props for that. He was just asking for it, and he not only had no cap, he had no muscles, either.

Lance looked like he might explode. I wondered who he'd explode at if he did: me or the kid? The kid, I decided. I'd already learned enough about Lance to know that. So I stepped between them.

"Get in the back of the line, dude," I said. "Or maybe you're hoping for a detention on your first day . . ."

He blew a fuse, but he didn't explode. I could see sparks in his eyes and his veins pulsing in his forehead.

He looked at Chase for help, but Chase just snickered. That had to hurt. I had come between him and his best friend.

"We'll save you a seat," I said to Lance.

He glared at me, then turned and stormed off.

"Thanks, dude," the kid said to me. "That's not how things usually go. Usually big guys like you stick together and have fun tormenting me."

I held out my hand. "I'm Enzo Harpold, and I'd appreciate your vote for class president."

"Hey! You're running, Enzo?" Chase said. "Me, too!"

"So am I," said the kid. "Giovanni Gordillo. And you guys don't stand a chance."

7. Onward Toward Glory!

The three of us sat together in the cafeteria along one of the mile-long, foldable, metal tables. Chase sat in the middle. He spent most of lunchtime turned toward me—and his back toward Lance—listening as I revealed a few details about my dad's job at Kap ("Whoa! Lucky you!" he said) and our tour of the western United States. I didn't say too much. I was creating interest. Building suspense. Whetting his appetite.

Lance mostly groaned and sighed and tried to get Chase's attention, or even to hear what I was saying. Mostly Chase said, "Shut up! I can't hear!"

One time, Chase leaned in close to me and whispered, "Do you see Misa over there?" He gestured with his eyes down the table from us to a group of squealing females in brand-new outfits and too much makeup. "She's the blond one with pink streaks."

I saw the one he meant. She was talking nonstop and waving her hands around and laughing real loud and sometimes doing little dances in her seat. She shimmied her shoulders and tossed her blond and pink hair for emphasis. She reminded me of Lupe, which put me right off my lunch.

"Yeah?" I said sourly.

"She's been stealing looks at you, then whispering things to her friends."

"So?"

"*So?* She was the cutest girl at San Joaquin last year, and she looks even better now."

I did a double take. "You into girls, dude?"

He got quiet.

"He's *totally* into them," Lance piped in. "He loves them, in fact."

Chase punched him.

"That hurt," Lance said, and socked Chase back.

"Ow! You used knuckles!" Chase said, and punched Lance back, harder.

"Will you boneheads knock it off?" I said. "How old are you anyway?"

"He hit me!" Lance whined.

"Exactly," I said.

I noticed Misa peeking at me. She blushed, then looked away. Her friends all went, "Ooooh!" Then they busted into high-pitched squeals.

Uh-oh. I was cute all right. I wasn't sure how much I hated it, though. Or if I hated it.

Kai stumbled up then, in his newborn-coltish way.

"Hey, Enz. What's up?" he said, setting his tray across from mine and starting to sit down.

Chase and Lance stared at him.

"Who's this, Enzo?" Lance asked with a smirk. "Friend of yours?"

I started to answer, but I didn't know how. I should have said, "Yeah, what about it?" But I felt ashamed. I wasn't proud of feeling this, but there was no denying I didn't want them to know Kai was my best friend. Or had been.

"I'm Kai," Kai said, and stuck out his hand, like he wanted five or something.

Lance's smirk grew. He looked at Kai's palm

like it was the last thing in the world he'd ever consider coming into contact with.

"Oops," Kai said, pretending he was embarrassed. "Forgot to say 'Simon says,' didn't I? *Simon says*, give me five."

Lance raised an eyebrow. "Still no, dude."

"Simon says, don't shake, then," Kai said. He waited a couple seconds, then pulled his hand back and chirped, "Thanks!"

I leaned across the table toward him. "*Enzo* says, knock it off, Kai," I said.

"You didn't say 'Simon says,' so I have to keep it up."

"I mean it, Kai . . . ," I growled.

"Simon says, don't hear my voice!" he said loudly. "*Burn!* You all heard me!" He laughed again, then dipped his corn dog into his mustard and stuffed it into his goofy mouth.

"Hey, do you know this guy, Enzo?" Chase asked.

"We went to Tuolomne together," I said.

"We've been best friends since first grade!" Kai said through his food. Fortunately, the corn dog muffled what he said.

"I'm done eating," I said, and stood up. "Let's go."

"Me, too," said Chase.

"What about your friend, Enzo?" Lance said, poking his thumb at Kai.

"Yeah!" Kai said, swallowing hard to clear his mouth. "I just got here!"

"Exactly," I said under my breath, loud enough for only Chase to hear.

Again, I felt bad, but what was I going to do? It wasn't my fault Kai was a dork, that he hadn't changed like I had.

Chase nudged me with his shoulder and snorted. He was laughing at Kai. And it made me feel worse.

I caught Lance staring me down, watching me squirm. He was loving it. Luckily, Chase didn't notice.

We walked away, into the Student Commons, an area with a bunch of couches and chairs and a high wall of windows looking out onto the parking lot. Lots of kids were in there, gabbing and checking everyone else out. Most of them looked older than us. I didn't see any familiar faces.

Till I saw my sister Lupe's painted face. She was chattering away with a gaggle of girls. She saw me, too, then turned away like she hadn't. She snubbed me, in other words, just like I had snubbed Kai. It didn't feel good.

"Let's go outside," I said to Chase.

Stan had no playground, of course. No kickball field. Not even hoops. I guess that meant by sixth grade you were supposed to have given up on fun stuff like that. Some kids had formed hacky sack circles, but most stood around, talking. A few kids had wandered off alone, with their lunches and their books. I guessed these were kids new to town or losers: kids with no old friends, kids who'd made no new friends that day, kids who never made friends.

I was relieved I'd attracted two new cool friends already. I wasn't sure if I should count Lance as a friend, but I knew that he'd at least try to hang out with me as long as Chase did. And Chase definitely liked me. Plus I'd been nominated class president. And girls were staring at me and whispering. Whether or not all that was good, it sure beat sitting alone on bleachers, nibbling a

PB&J or reading a book and trying to pretend it didn't bother you that you were alone.

And then I spotted Kai by himself on the bleachers. He was now eating a sandwich and jabbing at his cell phone. He wasn't calling anyone; he was playing a game. Probably Tetris. That was his favorite. He played it all the time. To me, trying to get all those boxes to fit together felt more like cleaning the garage than playing a game. I was glad he was too absorbed to see me.

"Let's go back inside," I said to Chase.

He laughed.

My next class was social studies. Lance was in it, as was Iris, Misa (the blonde who was peeking at me), and Kai. When me and Lance walked in, there weren't any two seats together, so we split up. This didn't bother either of us.

Kai eagerly pointed to a seat beside him where he'd set his backpack, and was whisper-chanting, "Enz! Enz! Enz!" I pretended not to notice. I saw a seat open next to Iris, but she still had that smug look on her face from the last time I saw her. There was an open seat in front of Misa, but I didn't want her behind me, staring at me and whispering all period. So I kept going and took a seat in the back of the room. It wasn't till I sat down that I realized the kid with the bow tie from the lunch line was sitting in the desk beside me.

"Hello, Enzo," he said.

I nodded at him.

"Maybe you don't remember me," he went on. "Giovanni Gordillo. My friends call me Gio. I'm the kid you defended in the lunch line today. The one who is running for class president against you? The one who is going to win, too, I'm afraid."

The kid just beamed at me. What was with him anyway? Didn't he know where he was? And whose idea was the bow tie? And the slicked-down hair with the part that exposed half an inch of scalp?

"Your name is short for something, I suspect," he said. "Are you Italian, by chance? My grand-parents emigrated from Italy . . ."

"Excuse me, Gio," I said, and stood up and moved over a couple rows. I'd had to shun my best friend for being a dork. I wasn't going to let an even dorkier kid attach himself to me like some sort of dork barnacle.

Kai, who was now a few seats in front of me, twisted around and was hissing and snapping his fingers, trying to get my attention. Lance was looking back and forth between Kai and me, and grinning. I knew what that meant: he was going to try to use Kai to ruin my standing with Chase.

Misa kept sneaking little peaks at me over her shoulder and blushing. Iris was looking over her shoulder at me, too—and down her nose.

I ignored all of them. I didn't like being a creep, but I told myself it wasn't my fault. Middle school did not reward people for basic human decency. In middle school, it was survival of the fittest. And I was pretty fit.

I had to remember that it was I who had been given the cap, and with it came great responsibilities. Owning the cap meant I needed to model excellence and attain glory. I could not let Kai drag me down. I couldn't let anyone do that. I had the cap. Greatness was my destiny.

My last class of the day was science, taught

by a Ms. Savjani. I had six teachers and five of them were female. Story of my life. I mean, come on!

Chase was in Savjani's class, too, and afterward he suggested we go to the skate park.

"Do you have a board?" he asked.

I was so glad he asked. Did I have a board? I had a cutting-edge Kap "anti-gravity" board, which Evan called "spring-loaded, for extra pop." The deck was razor-thin and light as air, and the logo and graphics looked as if they were part of the wood, not painted on. I could imagine his face when I showed it to him.

But I played it cool.

"Yeah," I said. "I have a board."

Lance walked up.

"You guys going to b-ball tryouts?" he asked.

I groaned. I wanted to show Chase my board. I wouldn't mind showing Lance, either.

"What? You don't play b-ball, Lorenzo? What do you play? Boring old baseball?"

I thought about my basketball gear: my Kap shoes, jerseys, shorts, socks. I had a ball signed by Kobe Bryant.

"No, I play," I said. "But Chase and I were just heading to the skate park."

That lit Lance up.

"Yeah, well, tryouts are now," he said to Chase, "so if you want to make the team . . ."

Chase nodded his head. "Yeah, I do." He looked at me. "We can go to the skate park any time, Enz. Right now, let's go show the Killer what we got."

It just so happened that some of what *I* got, I got from real, live NBA b-ballers: tips from pros in L.A., Frisco, Portland, and Seattle. Yeah, I wanted to show the Killer—and Chase and Lance and everybody—what I had learned from them.

But I decided to hide my eagerness. Be cool.

"All right," I said, and Chase brought up his fist for a bump. I bumped it. "Let's show him what we got."

Lance looked pleased, like he hoped he would mop the floor with me.

I was looking forward to disappointing him.

I'd never tried out for a school team before. There were tons of guys there wanting to make the cut. A lot of guys were not going to. Would I be one of them? I didn't think so. Not only was I in great shape and coached by the best in the game, I had the cap. I was unbeatable.

Basketball's a tough game. A player's in almost constant motion: running, dribbling, jumping, shooting, passing, rebounding, defending. You have to have strength, coordination, skill, and endurance. Some of the guys who were trying out had better jump shots or layups. Some were better ball handlers. But nobody outlasted me. I didn't dog a single drill.

This seemed to tick Lance off, which made him screw up a lot. I made a point of swiping the ball away from him whenever I could, especially when I sensed a coach watching. I even drew a couple of offensive fouls from him, which wasn't hard. He's pretty offensive.

Chase played pretty well, though he had a tendency to telegraph his moves. His fakes were a joke. I could have blocked most of his shots, stolen most of his passes, and beaten him to the basket any time I wanted. Instead, I avoided him. I didn't want to make him look bad. I didn't want him blaming me when he got cut, which I figured he would.

At the end of tryouts, Killer really ran us hard. We had to run from the baseline to every single painted line on the floor and back. Because the gym was used for so many different games, there were probably a hundred lines. Guys dropped like flies, wheezing and coughing. My lungs felt like they were on fire. My leg muscles turned to jelly. But I finished with my head up. Lance and Chase finished, too, then collapsed onto their knees.

We wouldn't know who'd made the team till the next day when they posted the names, but as I pulled on my cap in the locker room, I was pretty sure "Enzo Harpold" would be on that list.

"You still want to hit the skate park?" I asked Chase as we stepped outside in our street clothes, our hair all wet.

"Are you crazy?" Chase laughed. "No *way*! I'm exhausted, dude!"

"I'm still up for it," I said, though I was totally exhausted, too, and the last thing I wanted to do was more exercise. In other words, I was bluffing.

Lance glared at me. "Count me out, for sure. You coming, Chase?"

"Which way you going?" Chase asked me.

Oh, yeah. I forgot. Home. I had to get home. And the bus had left ages ago. And home was far away.

I nodded in the opposite direction they were going.

"All right, then," Chase said. "Catch you tomorrow, Enzo. I bet you'll be on Killer's list."

Lance grumbled, "Yeah, right," under his breath.

"Thanks," I said. "I bet you will be, too"—I glanced at Lance—"Chase."

Lance faked a smile, then erased it. "Come on, dude," he said, bumping Chase's shoulder with his own.

They walked away, smacking each other around like guys do.

I was alone. And a long way from home.

I took out my cell. An empty battery symbol flashed a few times, then the phone went dark again.

I adjusted my cap and started walking.

8. Slam Dunk

Usually I get home from the first day of school exhausted, depressed, bitter, and dreading the hundreds of school days ahead of me. But even after the long walk, I was in a pretty upbeat mood.

Mom, on the other hand, was a basket case.

"Where have you been?" she screeched when I walked through the door. She threw her arms around me and squeezed and kissed me desperately, as if I'd just run out of a burning building or something

"You weren't on the bus," Lupe chimed in. She was sitting on the new flowery, pink couch, and making the universally recognized face for *I got you so busted*!

When Mom finally released me, and my

blood started circulating again, I told her about basketball tryouts, then I spilled the whole day's events in one big rush of words. (Who cares about being cool around your mom?) She shrieked with joy and congratulations.

"I am not surprised," she said. "My strong, handsome, intelligent boy!"

Then she hugged the life out of me again.

Lupe fumed on the couch. Obviously, Miss Perfect had hoped I would fall flat on my face at Stan. Ha! Take that, Lupe!

Dinner wasn't ready, so I headed to the laundry room, took my sweaty gym clothes out of my duffel, dumped them in a hamper, then climbed the stairs to my two-toned room. The walls were still bare. I had decided not to rehang my old posters and stuff. Instead, I'd hang the new Kap stuff from the trip, including the real prize: an autographed, full-color, life-size photo of LeBron James, slam-dunking. I so looked forward to the day when I could slam dunk. I imagined it was at least a couple years off.

I took off my cap and set it on my dresser, visor pointing back at me. It was a bit worn, a little dirtier and sweatier. But its bill was still flat.

"Thanks, buddy," I said to it.

I ate a big dinner: three of my mom's beef empanadas, some carrot onion salad, and two bowls of ice cream for dessert. Probably because of the tryouts. And the walk home.

I hadn't gotten any homework, so I watched an A's game with my dad. He asked how my first day of middle school went.

"The rules are ridiculous," I said. "The bus ride stinks. Lupe was a total snob to me." I paused. "But it was pretty good."

"Oh, yeah?"

"I met a couple guys. Chase and Lance. One of them is pretty cool. Lance is out to get me."

"Already?"

"I think he thinks I'm trying to be Chase's new best friend."

"Are you?"

"I just met him. He's okay."

"And Kai?"

I sighed. "Kai still acts like a fourth grader."

"You guys have been friends an awful long time."

"Yeah, but this is middle school, Dad. There's a lot more guys to choose from."

Dad looked at me like a dad, like he knew everything about being a boy, because he'd been there, and there wasn't anything I could be thinking or feeling that he hadn't already thought and felt, and that he could easily set me straight and tell me exactly what I should do in order not to screw up, but he wasn't going to do that, because I had to figure stuff out for myself. He probably thought his being quiet right then did me more good than offering advice. But I wouldn't have minded the advice.

"Did you tell everyone about the trip?" he asked.

"Not very much," I said. "I want to make it last. And I don't want to sound too braggy. That'll turn people off."

Dad nodded. "I see."

We watched the game awhile, then I asked, "How's Evan? How's the job?"

"Good," Dad said. "Evan seems pleased with my work, at least."

"Of course he is. He thinks you're great."

"If you say so. I feel old down there. It's not the same as it was at G&W."

Duh! I thought. What was wrong with him?

After the game, as he got up to leave, he patted my shoulder and said, "Good luck tomorrow with the team. And with the election."

"Thanks," I said. "But, hey, don't mention my running for class president to Evan, okay?"

I made the team. All hail the cap!

Chase made it, too, which was kind of a surprise. I think he got picked because he tried so hard. Coach Keller gave him an A for effort.

And Lance? He got cut. I wasn't exactly crushed.

I also cleared the general election for class president on Friday. The top five vote getters would move on to the run-off election, in October. I was one of them. Chase wasn't. Neither was Giovanni.

All the candidates—including those for vice president, secretary, and treasurer—started campaigning, which mostly meant making and hanging posters and banners. Kyla, the girl in my homeroom who nominated me, volunteered to be my campaign manager, and got some of her friends to help her. It was fine by me. At least I didn't have to make any stupid posters or banners.

They came up with catchy slogans like:

ELECT ENZO!

ENZ FOR PREZ!

ENZO FOR PREZIDENZO!

THE ENZ JUSTIFIES THE MEANS!

Chase said Kyla worked so hard for me because she liked me, and a rumor to that effect started bouncing around the halls. Kyla instructed me not to deny the rumors. She told me to say, "No comment." She said rumors were publicity, and all publicity was good. But I thought she probably had a different agenda. Like Chase said, she liked me. I didn't like her back, of course. I just wanted to win the election. I guess I was using her. Wasn't that what politicians did?

One of my opponents challenged me to a debate. Kyla advised against it.

"You don't win school elections because of your positions on school issues," she told me.

"No? What do we win on?"

She just blushed, and said, "Cuteness."

Again, I went along. I didn't want to debate anybody. I wasn't really sure what my positions even were.

I got pretty excited as the election grew near. I enjoyed competition. I liked winning. And I figured I would win. With the cap, how could I lose?

All the candidates did have to give three-minute speeches during a class assembly in the gym. Kyla, again, instructed me to ignore the issues and just make the speech funny.

"Use a lot of popular expressions and gestures, repeat the slogans, get the crowd chanting, then get off the stage," she told me.

In the end, she wrote my speech for me. It was pretty funny. I wondered why she didn't just run for president herself. But I guess, secretly, I knew. She must not have had anything magical, like my cap. And she wasn't cute enough, either.

I did have to punch up the speech a bit. It was

too girly in places. Then I rehearsed it in front of the bathroom mirror at home. Sometimes the Sisterhood would bang on the door and yell things like, "There are other people in this house besides you, Mr. President!" and "I bet Abe Lincoln never spent this much time in the bathroom!" But I ignored them. My speech was important. I had to get it right.

I got pretty jittery the next day during the class assembly, waiting for my turn. We had to sit on folding chairs in the middle of the gym floor, facing the audience, who sat on the bleachers. I didn't even bother listening to the two candidates' speeches before mine. I knew who I was voting for. Plus I wanted to stay focused. I'd never prepared so hard for anything this school related in my life, and I wasn't even going to get graded on it. What was I doing? I thought about Evan, and how I was going against his advice about never running for office. I thought about bolting.

But I didn't. I stayed. I understood that my reputation depended on not quitting, and if I'd learned anything yet about middle school, it was that your rep was everything.

Finally, they called my name.

My fellow sixth graders started clapping. Some whooped and cheered. Kyla's crew, probably. One kid was doing one of those loud, fingers-in-your-mouth whistles. And I heard one hiss. Lance, probably. Or Kai?

I was wearing my best Kap gear, including the cap, of course. I wasn't sure if that was okay. I didn't see anybody in the audience wearing one. But I was onstage. Wasn't a person allowed to wear anything he wanted onstage? Under the circumstances, wasn't the cap part of my costume?

I decided right then my first act as president would be to repeal the no-caps-worn-in-school rule.

As I neared the microphone stand, I scanned the crowd. They were mostly smiling and clapping. I loved it. I suddenly understood my sister Desi in a whole new way. Being liked by so many people—being popular—felt amazing.

"No . . . thank you . . . thank you . . . please," I said, motioning for quiet. "No . . . that's too much . . . that's too much . . . thank you."

They got louder. I heard laughter, which gave me a real charge.

Kyla and her gang jumped to their feet and started chanting, "EN-ZO! EN-ZO! EN-ZO!"

I did the quiet gesture again: raising my palms and pumping them against the air, as if I were actually trying to push back their cheering.

"You're too kind . . . really . . . thank you . . . thank you . . ."

They got even louder. I could see our principal, Ms. Kish, out of the corner of my eye, getting ready to come over and silence everyone. I didn't want that. This was my crowd. My moment. I would silence them.

I lifted the mic from its stand and wandered closer to the audience. *My* audience. Like magic, they quieted down. I think it really was magic. The magic of the prototype. The magic of the cap.

"Can we talk?" I asked.

This wasn't the opening I'd rehearsed. It wasn't in the speech Kyla had written and I'd punched up. It had just come to me. Magically. And it got laughs. I decided then that I didn't need a script. I would put my trust in the cap. It would give me the words to say.

"Let's face it," I went on. "We're sixth graders. Which makes us, basically . . . well . . . punching bags. When an eighth grader has a bad day, he just picks on one of us, and then he feels a whole lot better."

I lowered the mic and made an exaggerated *What're-ya-gonna-do?* gesture. "So here I am, running for president of the sixth-grade class. In other words, I'm running for top punching bag. Why would a guy want to do such a thing?"

I shook my head.

"*You* wouldn't do such a thing. You're *not* doing such a thing. You're smart. Smarter than me. Only me and these guys"—I gestured at the other candidates behind me—"are *dumb* enough to run for top punching bag."

I glanced at Ms. Kish. She had her head tilted and was shaking it tightly at me, telling me to knock it off. I looked at Kyla. She was squinting at me, probably because I was straying from her precious script, but she was also smiling. I judged from the reactions of these two females that I was doing all right. So I went on.

"These other candidates have high hopes for us this year. They have big plans. They will make this the brightest, shiningest, most amazingest year ever . . . for every *punching bag at Stan*."

I was moving up and down the length of the bleachers, nodding and swaggering. I had these guys in the palms of my hands.

"What do I have?" I asked.

I scanned the crowd, as if I was hoping for an answer. I wasn't hoping for anything. I'd already decided what the answer to my question would be. I'd decided before I'd asked it. And it wasn't in the script.

"Do I have high hopes?" I asked. "Do I have big plans? What do I have?"

The audience got quiet and leaned in, waiting for my answer. I felt it. I felt them come to me. It was delicious.

"I have," I said, and pointed up, "a cap on my head."

There was an explosion then, a *BOOM!* of screaming, hooting, foot stomping, fist pumping, whistling, cheering—the works.

"I have a cap on my head . . . ," I added, ". . . *in school*!"

The crowd went nuts. Especially the guys. They started slamming into each other, making ape noises, slapping their hands together like seals.

I soaked it up for a while, then I raised my hands for silence. The crowd obeyed this time. They were mine. I glanced at Ms. Kish. She was not happy. Kyla was. I spotted Lance, his arms crossed, sulking. I was having a blast.

I lowered my hands. I cleared my throat. Then I spoke, slowly, solemnly:

"My first order of business as president of the proud . . . *brave* . . . sixth-grade class of Stanislaus Middle School"—I paused to hear the echo of my words. I heard a pen drop, ricochet around the supports under the bleachers, then hit the floor—"will be to *repeal the no-caps-worn-in-school rule*!"

The audience (mostly the guys) jumped to their feet. Someone (probably Kyla) started the chant up again: "EN-ZO! EN-ZO! EN-ZO! EN-ZO!"

I smiled and waved and bowed till Ms. Kish came over and made me sit down. It took her a while to get the crowd quiet.

After that, the presidency was a slam dunk.

9. Pep

Yes, I was elected president. Some cap, huh?

I knew Mom and Dad would be proud, but Desi—she just flipped. She couldn't believe I had gotten so popular so fast. I guess she must have thought I had been a major loser. It worked out pretty sweet, actually, not only because she stopped bossing me around so much, but also because whatever Desi did, Susana did. So I had two nice-ish sisters for a change.

Lupe was too busy being jealous to be happy for me. She got nominated for eighth-grade class president—as she had been in sixth and seventh—but, like in those years, she'd gotten weeded out in the general elections. With the other weeds. She didn't have the maturity, however, to see past her own failures and to congratulate her brother on his triumph. She was small that way. It was probably one of the reasons she'd never won the presidency. Which I did on my first try.

And Nadine? I didn't bother telling her I'd been elected. I figured she would have a problem with it somehow, like she did with most things that had to do with normal people doing normal things.

My campaign manager, Kyla, acted as if my election made us, like, boyfriend-girlfriend. Which was crazy. When she started telling people we were going out, I had to set her straight. I caught her one day at her locker. She was yakking with a couple of girls from my campaign crew.

"You been telling people we're going out?" I asked her. "Because we're not."

Her mouth fell open, and then her eyes got all wet. Her friends hooked her arms, as if she was going to collapse or something.

"I never said we were going out," I said. "You're the one who nominated me. I didn't ask you to. I didn't ask you to make posters or write a speech, either. You wanted to."

Her chin started quivering. One of her friends whispered comforting words in her ear, all the while glaring at me like I was a criminal.

"I didn't—" Kyla started to say, but the words stuck in her throat. She swallowed and started again in a shaky voice. "I didn't t-tell anyone that."

Her glaring friend added, "She knows you don't like her that way. She knows you just *used* her to get elected."

"Used her? Ha!" I said, though that was pretty much true. It wasn't personal, though. It was political. And it sure didn't give her the right to pretend we were going out.

After that, Kyla stopped talking to me, or acknowledging me in any way, which didn't bother me one bit. Then word got out that she was trash-talking me, and that did bother me. I didn't confront her about it, though. I just sucked it up. A president can't expect to be loved by everyone. Or—let's be frank here—to love everyone.

The student council met every other Thursday. Misa, the blonde with the pink streaks who Chase said crushed on me, was vice president, Iris was elected treasurer, and another girl,

Cassie (she and Misa were both cheerleaders), was secretary. Me and three girls. Sound familiar?

The meetings were a total drag. It wasn't in my power to make any important decisions, even though I was president. I had a vote and all, but it counted exactly the same as the others. I thought it would count at least triple. And I couldn't veto the principal's or the school board's decisions. I couldn't make changes to school policies or the schedule or the budget. I couldn't fire teachers. I couldn't even repeal the no-caps-worn-in-school rule. I didn't have any real power at all. The whole election turned out to be a total joke, one of those stunts adults pull to get kids thinking they have power in their lives. The school gods wanted us to believe that school was like real life, when they knew the elections were a fake.

The council's only actual job was to raise money for our class, which meant devising and organizing events like car washes, raffles, bake sales, and boring carnivals with no rides. I thought I was going to die of boredom. Evan had been right. I should have never run for elected office. Lesson learned the hard way.

The only good part about being president was getting to *be* president. Having the title. President Enzo Harpold. *¡Enzo Prezidenzo!* From then on, I got introduced at most class assemblies, and some school body assemblies. The sixth-graders would rabbit-punch the air like boxers, because of the punching bag bit in my speech, and the crowd would go berserk. Ms. Kish would always quiet everyone down with a threat of some kind, then glare at me. It was in those moments that I enjoyed being president.

Word had begun to spread about my trip, all my cool gear, and all the famous people I'd met. Plus I'd made the basketball team. All this had transformed me into an overnight sensation, a middle-school superstar.

To my surprise, I loved it. Even the attention from girls. I let them love me; I just didn't let them near me. (Well, none of them except Analisa, who I'll talk about in a minute.) I actually looked forward to going to school each day. I had school spirit. I had pep. Strange but true.

I had to keep my grades up to stay on the team, so I listened a bit more carefully during class. This was not easy with all the notes girls kept sending to me. I studied some at night in my room, after basketball practice and dinner. Sometimes Dad helped me. Sometimes Mom did. Sometimes *Desi* did. All this help did the trick: I kept my grades up.

The team practiced throughout September and October, gearing up for our first game in November. Coach Keller said we were in a tough division, very competitive, so he pushed us hard. Even though I knew I was a lock for the starting five, I gave 110 percent during practice. I was getting used to getting most of the things I wanted then and was willing to do whatever was necessary to get the rest. I owed it to myself, and to the cap.

The cheerleading squad practiced in the gym at the same time the team did, wearing their short, pleated, red-and-white skirts and red-and-white sweaters, chanting and clapping and flipping. Sometimes, they would chant my name—"*E!* E-N-Z-O! *He!* He's our man, O! *On!* On offenzo!"—and I would feel . . . I don't know . . . sort of electrified. Energized. It helped my game.

There were four cheerleaders in all. Besides Misa and Cassie, there was Mackenzie, who was in my science class and was always mean and sarcastic, and a girl I didn't have in any classes, Analisa.

Rumor had it that Analisa crushed on me, too, but I didn't believe it. Of the girls on the squad, she was the one least interested in boys, and the most interested in sports. She was the only one I'd ever had a normal conversation with.

Kap was her favorite brand, so, after hearing about my trip, she came up to me and gushed about how lucky I was that my dad worked there. She wanted to hear every detail about the trip, and, though I'd promised myself I wouldn't, I told her everything. I think it was because she was so totally awestruck by every word I said, more awestruck than anybody else I'd talked to. She kept saying "No *way*!" in this breathless way that I liked. And she knew all about Kap, and was so jealous of all the sports I got to try, and the sports stars I got to meet, and when I showed her where LeBron James signed my cap, I swear she almost fainted.

"That's the most amazingest cap ever," she said.

Yeah, we kind of spoke the same language.

But there was no crushing going on. I want to make that perfectly clear. She didn't have a crush on me, and I certainly did not crush on her. I don't crush on anyone. I don't crush. In fact, I hate crushing.

In fact, just because Misa crushed on me and Chase crushed on her, Chase got all sore at me. Like I did anything! It wasn't my fault. I didn't ask to be cute. I hated being cute. So it was totally stupid for Chase to get mad at me for what stupid Misa felt. I never encouraged her. Once I found out, in fact, I started acting really rude and obnoxious to her on purpose, but it didn't cool her off one bit.

Chase also got bent out of shape when Coach announced I would be starting and Chase wouldn't be. I tell you what, it's tough being cute and excellent at sports. I started understanding what guys like David Beckham and A-Rod went through. Getting adored by people you don't know can be cool, but it can make things uncomfortable with people you do know. Chase, for example. And Kai and Lance, and Misa and Kyla. Some people just can't deal with other people's success.

Chase acted like a big baby the day of our first game. We had to dress nice and wear a tie to school on game days, and, right in front of Chase, Misa said I looked handsome. Ugh. But you know what Chase did? After she walked away, he punched me. What did *I* do?

When Coach introduced us at the pep rally, the cheerleaders ran out and did cartwheels and flips. Then Coach introduced us, one at a time, starters first. I got the biggest response. Kids hooted and whooped and yelled and did the rabbit-punching thing. Misa did about a million handsprings down the court, ending with this amazing aerial thing, but, for Chase's sake, I didn't so much as clap.

When the rally was over, we hit the locker room. Chase ignored me. I ignored him back. I changed back into my street clothes, including my tie—which, by the way, does not go with Kap wear. I grabbed my backpack and slipped it over my shoulder. Then I reached up for my cap.

It wasn't there.

I dug my hand deeper into the top shelf of my locker.

Nope.

I got up on my toes and stuck my face in. No cap.

I felt needle pricks of panic down my spine.

I pulled off my backpack, unzipped it, and groped around inside. I turned it upside down and dumped everything out. No cap.

"What's up?" asked River, our center, whose locker was next to mine.

I didn't answer. My tongue was frozen in fear.

I dropped my empty backpack and started searching the room.

"What you looking for, Enz?" guys kept asking me, but I shrugged them off.

After I'd scoured the locker room, I ran out into the gym. Everyone was already gone. I ran around, frantic, looking, looking. On the bleachers. Under the bleachers. I retraced my steps. I went back to my social studies room, and looked under my desk, under all the desks. People kept asking me what was wrong, if I'd lost something. I didn't answer.

Back in the hall, I tried to remember where I took it off, where I set it down. I remembered carrying it into the locker room, putting it on the shelf of my locker, shutting the door . . .

Someone must have swiped it. Yeah. Someone in the locker room. One of the guys, probably.

Chase, probably. He was sore at me.

I speed-walked back to the gym in a cold sweat. If someone stole it, I would have to catch him before he got away. I probably had already let him get away. I walked faster.

The locker room was empty. Everyone was gone.

I opened Chase's locker. No cap. I opened a couple of others. It was no use. I broke down. I fell to my knees. Tears squirted out of my eyes. My tongue unfroze.

"NOOOOOO!" I wailed, like a girl.

10. UnKapped

Coach appeared from somewhere. Had he been in his office this whole time? Had he seen me looking in other guys' lockers? Had he heard me bawling like a baby girl?

"Something wrong, Enzo?" he asked in his deep, manly voice. Coach had this way of talking that made a guy snap to attention and want to salute.

I shot to my feet. I didn't salute, though I did raise my hand to my face—to wipe away my girlish tears.

"No, sir," I said, my spine stiff. "My ca— I—I lost something."

"Something important?"

Important? Only the magic cap that made my life a dream come true.

But Coach was not the guy to explain this to. He was tough as nails. Hyper-serious. He wouldn't buy the magic-cap business, or that any cap, magic or not, was worth blubbering about, especially if you were a starter on his basketball team.

"No," I said. "Nothing important."

He gave me a quick nod, satisfied with this answer, then strode away in his crisply creased slacks. (He had to dress up on game days, too.)

I ran to the Lost and Found. The cap wasn't there.

I asked around. No one had found it. No one had seen it. That was because it was gripped in the dastardly thief's villainous clutches.

There would be no point asking my dad for another cap. It was a prototype, a model of a cap that wasn't even available to the public yet. There couldn't have been many of those lying around, waiting to be handed out to new employees' kids, especially to those kids who had already lost one. And even if Evan did find me another prototype, what were the chances it would be lucky? I mean, Kap couldn't be making lucky caps on purpose.

Could they?

Maybe Dad would get in trouble if Kap found out I lost their prototype—the secret cap they stupidly trusted me with. Maybe he'd even get fired!

Maybe, I thought to myself, I shouldn't be running around telling everyone I'd lost it. What if Lupe got word of it? She'd go right to Dad.

I decided not to report the cap missing to the office or to the police or the FBI. Other than Evan and the people at Kap, no adults would care anyway. They would say that it was just a hat and that there was nothing they could do about it. Adults have screwed-up priorities.

No, I was on my own. I was going to have to solve the case myself.

Obviously, someone stole the cap. But who? There was a school filled with suspects. I started a list:

Chase was at the top because he was mad at me, because Misa liked me instead of him, and because I was starting instead of him.

Then came Lance, who would have stolen it

because he hated me, because Chase was mad at me, or both.

Kai also could have done it. He felt rejected and abandoned. I hadn't seen him in the crowd during the rally. But, then again, he's so short I could have missed him.

Kyla felt rejected, too, and was bad-mouthing me. Would she have gone into the boys' locker room out of spite? Yeah, probably.

Iris might have arranged it as a gag, to teach me a lesson, to bring me down a peg. It was a long shot, but not out of the question.

Giovanni? How mad was he that I'd beaten him out for president? Mad enough to steal the thing that got me elected? Without a doubt.

And the other candidates for class president?

And the other forwards who had hoped to be starters?

And all those people who loved the cap— in other words, everyone? Including Analisa. Especially Analisa.

Who knows? Maybe Evan found out I ran for class officer against his advice and decided to take the cap back in retaliation.

Okay, maybe that was far-fetched. But even without him, I had a really long list of suspected thieves.

I decided to start at the top of it, with Chase. He had been in the locker room around the time of the theft. As second-string forward, he would benefit from me not having my cap for the game that night. And he was sore at me because a girl he liked liked me. He looked mighty guilty.

He was also technically my best friend. But was he? Maybe all he had ever wanted from me was the cap.

I made up my mind right then: Chase was the thief.

I had till game time to find where he hid it; otherwise, I would be luckless for the game.

The team, the coach, the managers, the statisticians, the cheerleaders, and the driver boarded the bus after school. I didn't ignore anyone, but I didn't speak to anyone, either. This seemed fine with Chase. He was mad at me. The feeling was mutual. When we did make accidental eye contact, he squinted and looked away.

A fan bus followed us to the game so we'd

have a cheering section in Lardo. Even so, the reaction when our starters were announced over the loudspeaker was nothing compared to when the Wranglers' names were called out. The whole gym rattled. Too bad our first game had to be on the road.

We got the ball at the jump. River tipped it to Ryan, who brought it down court and passed off to me. I faked a pass, and the guy on me got caught flat-footed, leaving me an open path to the hoop. I broke by him, but somehow, instead of the floor, I bounced the ball off my foot, and it ricocheted into the stands. The crowd laughed.

The lucklessness had begun.

"Get back on D! Back on D!" Coach yelled over the laughter.

We set up our defense down on the Wranglers' end of the court. My guy danced around, trying to get open.

"Hey, bro," he said to me as he danced. "You know this is basketball, not soccer, right?"

Ha-ha.

Pop. The ball was in his hands. He spun one way, then another, then broke for the basket. I drifted back, trying to stay between him and the hoop, and backed into a Wrangler setting a pick. My guy made an easy layup.

Someone blasted a horn, and the Wrangler cheerleaders cheered for their guy: "J-A-C! C-O-B! He's the man! The man for me!"

Man? What was he—eleven?

He snickered at me when I caught up with him downcourt.

"I have a feeling this is not going to be your night," he said.

I had the same feeling.

I missed my first four jump shots. I missed two free throws after Jacob fouled me. I fouled him three times in the first period, which, after he sank all his free tosses, gave his team six points. Then I missed my next three jump shots. I also was called for double dribbling, traveling, and three seconds in the lane. Then I got pulled for a sub: Chase.

He pulled off his warm-up jacket and ran onto the court. Did he give me an encouraging look as we passed each other, or a "You'll get 'em next time, buddy!"? Nope. He was totally stoked and shot me a sit-down-and-watch-how-this-game-is-really-played-sucka! smirk.

I could only gasp at the depth of his treachery. And give him props. He had planned it beautifully.

He played better than I'd ever seen him play. His jump shot couldn't miss. He made great moves under the basket: passing, rebounding, blocking shots, intercepting passes. He had game. But, of course, he had the cap.

We ended up winning the game by six points. I cheered as best I could, but it was difficult hiding my resentment. In the locker room, the guys were all loud and happy. I gritted my teeth watching them high-fiving and knuckle-bumping Chase, who'd had a great game. I fired eye daggers at him whenever I could. He shot them right back.

Our fans, including the cheerleaders, mobbed us when we stepped out of the locker room. Misa was in front and went straight for (wait for it) Chase. So *that's* how it was—she crushed on whoever was up at the time. Chase looked like a kid on Christmas morning who'd gotten everything he'd asked Santa for.

Analisa was the only one who came up to me.

"Don't look so glum," she said. "It isn't sports-manlike."

Did I look glum? I'd really been trying to look thrilled and triumphant.

"You probably heard about my cap, right?" I whispered out of the side of my mouth.

"I heard you were looking for it. Didn't you find it?"

I glanced around for eavesdroppers, then whispered in her ear, "Somebody *stole* it."

I wondered why I kept telling her things I'd decided not to tell anyone. Especially considering she was on my list of suspects.

"Noooo!" she breathed, and set her fingers on my arm. "Oh, Enz, that's terrible. I'm *so* sorry."

She seemed to mean it, and it felt good to have someone actually grasp the enormity of the tragedy, to have someone really understand what I was going through, that my eyes teared up. I quickly dabbed them with the sleeve of my hoodie.

"Who do you think it was?" she whispered, glancing around.

I glared at Chase. Misa was being extremely chummy, and he was eating it up.

"Chase?" Analisa asked. "But he's your friend."

"Why do you think he played so well tonight? And I played so lousy?"

"You don't believe . . ." She stopped to rephrase. "You don't really think you play so well because of a cap, do you?"

I leaned in close to her and whispered, "It's a lucky cap. It possesses magic."

It was such a relief to finally tell someone. And bizarre that I had done so to a girl.

"Oh, come on, Enz," she said, her head tilted. "Magic?"

"You don't get it. I was *nothing* before I got the cap. Nothing!" I hung my head. "And now I'm nothing again."

Analisa stifled a giggle.

"It's true!" I said. "I have to get it back! I have to! He must have hidden it. He can't wear it. Not at Stan. Not around anyone who goes to Stan. It's one of a kind, and he knows it. It's a prototype, you know."

"Prototype," Analisa said. " Yes, you told me."

"He must have the cap with him somewhere.

I don't think the magic works long distance. Anyway, I always kept it close by when I couldn't wear it."

"You're crazy. It's not the cap that makes you good at basketball."

"I'm going to find it. Will you help me?"

"I guess. I'm not going to do anything wrong, though. I don't want to get in trouble."

"You think I do? I just want to get back what is rightfully mine."

"So what do we do first?"

I checked for eavesdroppers, then whispered, "Check his duffel."

"You can't break into his personal property."

"He broke into *my* personal property. He *stole* my personal property!"

"You don't know that, and even if you did, two wrongs don't make a right."

"What do you suggest then?"

"Have you asked him if he took it?"

Girls! Talking is always their solution.

"So you think Chase would say, 'Oh, your cap, Enzo? Oh, yeah, sure . . . I took that. Why do you ask?'"

Analisa didn't appreciate the sarcasm.

"No, I didn't ask him," I said. "He hasn't been talking to me for a while now because of Misa. And because he's sore that I got picked to start instead of him. Now he's got his precious Misa and the cap, so he'll probably start the next game, too."

Analisa checked out Chase and his admirers, including Misa.

"I don't think he knows it's lucky," I said. "He probably just thinks I stunk tonight because I was upset about losing it. It's very important, Analisa, that he never finds out that the cap has magic. No one must ever find out."

She chuckled. "I'll never tell anyone about it."

"The guys all put their duffels out by the bus to be stowed. I should have a couple minutes to check out Chase's . . ."

"Don't do it, Enzo. I'm telling you, it's a mistake."

I was grateful for her concern. But I had to get the cap.

"Wish me luck," I said, and rushed away.

11. Interrogation of the Cheerleaders, Part One

The cap was not in Chase's duffel. But I got caught while I was looking for it in Chase's duffel. By Chase. He made such a big stink about it, I got called into Coach's office the next day.

"Why did you get into Chase's duffel?" Coach asked me after I sat down. No beating around the bush when it came to this guy.

"I was . . . looking for something," I tried.

"The something you 'lost' yesterday?" he asked. He didn't wait for me to answer. "Did you suspect Chase of taking something that belonged to you?"

How had he figured all this out? Was he some sort of genius? Or psychic? Or maybe wizard? Good or bad?

"No, sir," I lied.

"This something you 'lost,' did you lose it during the pep rally?"

"Yes."

"Was it in your locker?"

"Yes." At least I thought it was.

"I saw someone else in the locker room during the rally," Coach said. "Near your locker, as a matter of fact."

"You *did*?" I gasped. "Who?"

"I was ducking back into my office for my clipboard, and I was surprised to see someone in here . . ."

"And he was near my locker?" I could barely breathe.

"*She* was. It was one of the cheerleaders. I'm not certain which. I only saw her from behind. She was running for the door to the hall."

My mind crashed. Then rebooted. Then raced.

Why didn't he tell me this yesterday? When he found me bawling on the floor? If he was such a genius, why hadn't he put two and two together?

And why was a cheerleader in the boys' locker room? And why right before a pep rally? And why by my locker? Was she *in* my locker? Did she take my cap?

What would a cheerleader want with my cap? More important, *which* cheerleader would want my cap?

Misa, maybe. She had a crush on me. Maybe she wanted something of mine. Something dear to me. Would she want it enough to go into the boys' locker room? During a pep rally?

How about Mackenzie? She loved pranks. But this was pretty crazy even for her.

Cassie? The student council secretary? I couldn't think of a single reason why.

Analisa? No! She would never do that to me.

Would she?

She was a girl, after all, and it was a girl who was in the locker room, and girls were definitely not to be trusted.

I wished Coach had gotten a better look.

"Listen, Enzo," he said, "if something of yours was taken on school property, you should report it."

No way, I thought. No squealing. A guy is dead if he squeals.

"I think I just misplaced it."

"Can you tell me what it was so I can keep an eye out for it?"

"Uh . . . ," I said, trying to think of a reason not to tell him.

"I see you're wearing a new cap today," he said.

It was true: I was wearing one of my backup caps, a truly amazing one, a Kap cap, of course, but not a prototype. Not lucky or magic. Not to my knowledge, anyway. I'd never worn it. Why would I?

"So was it that fine cap you usually wear that you, uh . . . *misplaced*?" he asked.

He definitely possessed super mental powers of some kind. There was no point fighting him. I nodded.

"And you thought your friend Chase took it and hid it in his duffel," he said—not asked. He had everything all figured out.

I nodded again.

"I'm afraid that will cost you a lunch detention," he said.

My heart fell from my chest down into one of my feet. Detention? *Detention?* What happened to the think time? Didn't that come first? Why the bold leap straight to detention?

"Remember," Coach went on, "according to school rules, three detentions disqualifies you from participating in school sports. So be careful."

I gasped. Disqualify? No team?

"Also, I want to see you here after last period today. Since the incident happened on a sports-related trip, you will receive a separate consequence."

I nearly passed out. Really. I don't know how I stayed conscious. I wasn't exactly a saint, but I wasn't used to getting into this kind of trouble.

"You will need to apologize to the team. You will also need to write formal apologies to the principal of Lardo Middle School and to Ms. Kish."

I gulped. Aloud.

"I'll have some extra wind sprints for you," he added. "And that's all." Then he looked down at some papers on his desk.

The meeting was over. Time for me to leave.

"C-Coach," I said, then wished I hadn't. But I needed to know. "Will I be st-starting next F-Friday?"

"No," he said. Not "I'm sorry," or "I'm afraid not." Just "No." Firm. Direct. Final.

"Thanks, Coach," I said, and left.

Detention is sitting somewhere you don't want to be sitting, usually for an hour.

I sat and ate my lunch in the Detention Center. I sat with other detainees, as the Detention Center supervisor called us. They weren't hardened criminals or anything. Just kids. Boys and girls. Mostly boys.

We were released when the bell rang. I walked (not ran—I did not want to get into more trouble) toward the Student Commons. I hoped to talk to Misa before the next period started. I found her among a clump of chattering girls.

"Misa!" I called, and ran over to them.

The girls shut up at once and stared. Then they started whispering and tittering.

"Oh, hi, Enzo," Misa said without a drop of

enthusiasm. What happened here? Where was the dopey smile, the embarrassing compliments, and the getting too close to me all the time? What happened to that crush of hers? Did crushes evaporate, *poof*, just like that? Having no real experience with them, I couldn't say.

Apparently, though, they could be shifted, like a sniper changes targets. Misa now targeted Chase. Maybe she was behind the heist after all. Maybe she stole the cap because she was mad at me for not crushing on her back. Maybe she then handed it to Chase to win him over, which was why he played so well. Which was why she started crushing on him! *Which was why she stole the cap!*

Wait. That couldn't be right.

"Can I talk to you?" I asked.

The girls giggled.

"Sure," Misa said. "Go on. Talk."

More giggling.

"I meant *alone*," I said.

"Oh," she said, pretending to catch on when she'd known exactly what I'd meant all along. "But it's almost time for the late bell to ring . . ."

"It'll only take a second," I said, and reached out to take her arm.

"Hey!" she said, pulling it away. "Not so grabby!"

"Ooh, Chase won't like that," one of the girls said.

"Come on, Misa," I said, reaching for her arm.

She slapped my hand.

"Ow!" I said, though it didn't really hurt. Why do girls get to hit guys whenever they want?

"I'm not going *any*where with you, Mr. Grabby," she said. "In fact, if you don't leave me alone this instant, you will find yourself in a lot of trouble."

Trouble? I didn't want that. I took a step back.

"What's the matter with you?" I whined. "I mean, you *liked* me, like, yesterday!"

The girls all thought this was very funny.

"So why were you in the boys' locker room during the pep rally, Misa?" I asked in a loud, clear voice.

The girls stopped giggling and gaped at me. Misa's face turned red, which was as good as a confession to me.

"Coach Keller saw you," I announced.

"Coach Keller?" she asked, her voice breaking slightly.

The girls started whispering.

"He saw a cheerleader by *my* locker," I said.

Misa peeked around at her friends as if she didn't know how to answer this, what to say in front of them, whether or not they believed me. Then she laughed.

"But how would I even know which locker was *yours*?" she asked.

Hmm. I hadn't thought of that.

"Coach Keller must have made a mistake," she said. "Maybe he saw a cheerleader, but it wasn't me. I've never been in a boys' locker room in my life. And hope I never will!"

The girls answered, "Yeah!"

"Well . . . ," I said slowly. "I suppose Coach didn't say it was you *exactly*. I just figured it was you because . . . well . . . because you . . . you know . . . *liked* me."

"I *knew* you didn't know what you were talking about!" Misa laughed. "Let's go, girls!"

They all spun around and marched off, honking like geese.

That had not gone well.

I still believed Misa had been the cheerleader in the locker room, though. How was I going to prove it?

Process of elimination, maybe. I would talk to the other cheerleaders and see if they acted guilty, find out if they had alibis.

Misa, Cassie, Lance, Kai, and Iris were in my next class—social studies. Cassie wasn't there yet. I sat by Iris.

"Hello, juvenile delinquent," she said.

"How'd you hear about it?"

"It's all over school. You broke into your best friend's duffel bag. You got busted. Now he has your spot on the team, and the class president had to go to jail."

"Shut up," I said. She was talking pretty loud.

Cassie came through the door and took a seat in the front row, like always. I didn't have time to talk to her before the bell rang. I'd have to wait till after class.

I worried during class instead of paying attention to the teacher. My parents didn't know about the duffel incident, or the detention, or Coach's "consequences." This was a lot bigger trouble than I'd ever gotten into before. I didn't know how they were going to take it. I also didn't know if any of it went on my permanent record, if it would hurt my chances of working for Kap someday. I sure hoped not.

Lance turned to sneer at me quite a few times. He didn't bother hiding his hatred anymore. He let it breathe. It was like he thought I deserved it. Why? Because I peeked into Chase's bag. Big deal. Chase stole my cap.

Or did he? Maybe he'd put his goon Lance up to the job. Lance would have jumped at the chance to hurt me. He went to the game on the fan bus. Maybe he had the cap with him, which was how Chase got so lucky during the game. Maybe Lance kept it in his school locker. I thought maybe I should check and see . . .

No. I couldn't break into anyone else's stuff. Too risky. But boy, did I want a peek in that slimy creep's locker . . .

Kai sat a couple seats over from Lance. He stared at me till I looked over at him. His name was on my suspect list, too, but I realized right then he couldn't possibly have taken the cap. Kai was incapable of doing anything dangerous or illegal. He was so terrified of getting into trouble that some nights he couldn't sleep because he was so worried he'd accidentally committed a crime that day.

Besides, he could never have done something so low to me. Me and him went way back. Maybe things weren't like they used to be, and maybe he was sore about that, but we still had a bond. We actually did the blood-brother, pinprick thing when we were little. Kai would never hurt me the way the scum-sucking scumbag who stole my cap did. No way. Not my blood brother.

I was so sure he couldn't have stolen it, in fact, that I began to wonder if I should make him my top suspect. Isn't it always the least likely person in crime stories who ends up being the culprit?

Trying to think like a criminal was tricky.

I almost missed the way things were before the cap. Life was simpler then. Less drama. Less excitement. Less fun. But less girls. Less trouble.

Less worries. I wondered if it wouldn't be too long before I'd be living that life again. I wondered if Kai would ever forgive me for being such a stuck-up jerk and be my best friend again. Of course he would. What other choice would he have?

Class finally ended, and I caught up with Cassie in the hall. She stepped away from me when I said hi, like she was scared of me.

"What's wrong?" I asked.

"Nothing," she lied.

Something was definitely up. Was she feeling guilty? Or was I just too eager to talk to her? I'd never just walked up to her and said hi before. I barely even talked to her during class officer meetings. No one did. She just sat there and took minutes. For a cheerleader, she was pretty shy. I really couldn't imagine her ever going into a boy's locker room. Still . . .

"Did you go into the boys' locker room before the pep rally yesterday?" I asked. I wanted to put it out there fast and see how she reacted.

She scrunched up her nose like she smelled something stinky, and said, "WHAT? The *boys'* locker room? Why?"

I was wasting my time. She wasn't the thief.

"Why would you even *think* of something like that?" she asked. "Are you crazy or something?"

People were turning to look. I wanted to get out of there. I didn't need any more gossip and rumors.

"Never mind, sorry," I said, and slipped away into the crowd.

Mackenzie was in my fifth-period science class. She never ever gave a straight answer. I didn't expect to learn a thing from her. But I had to try.

I found her outside the lab.

"Mackenzie?" I called.

She turned. "Enzo?"

"Can I talk to you?

"I don't know. Can you?"

"No, seriously . . ."

"I didn't take it."

"What?"

"Your precious cap. Nor did I visit the boys' locker room."

Word travels at the speed of light at Stan.

"Anything else?" she asked.

I couldn't think of anything.

"Didn't think so," she said.

"No, wait. I do have one question."

"Okay, shoot."

"Did you see one of the *other* cheerleaders go into the locker room?"

"Yes," she said. Then she walked away.

"Wait!" I called after her. "Which one?"

She stopped. "You said you had *one* question. And I answered it."

"Give me a break."

"Where would you like it? Arm? Leg? *Skull?*" She grinned, pleased with her wit.

"Please, Mackenzie? Who was it?" I was begging. It was embarrassing.

"Lovely chatting with you," she said, and pranced away to the lab.

I considered following her, badgering her, but I doubted she'd crack. If, in fact, she had even seen a cheerleader go in there. You could never be sure with her. She loved twisting words around till your head was spinning.

Could *she* have been the one who went in? I doubted it. For one thing, why would she? For another, she'd never be caught dead in a boys' locker room. She didn't like boys about as much as I didn't like girls.

Then again, she was friends with Kyla, my bitter former campaign manager. Could she have used her locker room access and gone in and stolen my cap to help Kyla wreak her revenge on me for rejecting her?

I filed that away in my very messy brain. (Sometimes I wished I had a secretary or a janitor up there to clean and organize.) Then I went back to my list.

The only cheerleader left to interrogate was Analisa. She'd be in the gym after school. Maybe I could talk to her after our practices.

Analisa had acted horrified when I told her I thought someone had stolen my cap, but maybe that was just what she had done: *acted*. Like I said, she loved that cap more than anyone—except me, of course.

But she couldn't have stolen it. She was too nice to me.

Then again, wouldn't that be exactly what she would want me to think? Maybe she didn't like me at all. Maybe all she really liked about me was my cap.

Sure! She probably thought I was too dumb to figure it out. But I wasn't dumb. I'd figured it out.

Analisa was the thief!

12. Interrogation of the Cheerleaders, Part Two

"It was lousy of me to go into Chase's duffel," I said to the team, who Coach had huddled up to listen to me. "I'm sorry."

The guys shifted their weight from foot to foot in boredom and awkwardness. Except Chase. The apology wasn't working on him. What was he so mad about? He got everything he wanted. So I unzipped his bag—big deal!

After I apologized to the team, I had to sit down and write out the apologies to the principals of Lardo Middle School and Stan. While I was doing that, the team stretched. The cheerleaders did the same on their side of the gym: Misa, Cassie, Mackenzie, and the traitor-thief, Analisa.

When I finished the apologies, I joined in on the practice. I was so distracted, though, that

I messed up every play I was in. Not having the cap didn't help. I had never played worse, which was not going to get me back in the starting five.

No one talked to me in the locker room after practice, especially Chase. I told myself I didn't care. Who needed friends who like you only when you're on top, who dump you like a hot potato when you're down, friends with no loyalty whatsoever?

Friends like me.

I understood then why it just might have been Kai who stole the cap. I had been a bad friend to him. He would have been right to try to drag me down a couple notches.

"Any luck?" Analisa asked. We were back in the gym, back in our street clothes, and she was looking super concerned and sympathetic. The big actress.

I shook my head, going along with her little pretend play. I figure she'd let on more if she didn't know I knew she was the cap thief.

"Both Chase and Lance are acting pretty suspicious," I said. "Misa, too. Did I tell you that

Coach Keller told me that he saw a cheerleader in our locker room just before the pep rally?"

I watched her the way I watched LeBron James when he showed me some of his moves: with intense focus. She faked a passable look of surprise bordering on shock. I bet she practiced making looks of surprise bordering on shock at home in front of the mirror.

"So you think it was Misa?" she asked.

Clever. Trying to shift the blame.

"No," she corrected herself. "She crushed on you."

"Maybe she was after a souvenir," I offered.

"And now she likes Chase?"

"I guess."

"Maybe she liked him all along. Maybe she was only pretending to like you."

Analisa had a suspicious mind. Like me. And she was highly logical. Also like me. That might have been why I liked her. Part of me wanted her to slip and give herself away as the thief. Another part wanted her to do something that would prove she was innocent.

"She denies going in," I said, "but I don't believe

her. She acted really guilty. Cassie and Mackenzie said they didn't go in, either, but I believed them. They didn't really have a motive anyway."

Analisa wrinkled her brow, like she was thinking hard about something, or maybe worrying, or maybe dreaming up more backstabbing schemes. Who knew what girls thought?

"So you grilled the other cheerleaders and now it's my turn, huh?" she asked at last. She was angry. Or was she pretending to be mad to hide her guilty feelings?

"Huh?" I said.

"You're grilling me," she said, getting madder every second. "You think I went into the locker room."

"No, no," I said. Real or fake, her anger made me uncomfortable. She'd never been mad at me before.

"Maybe it wasn't a cheerleader," she said. "Maybe Coach made a mistake."

Was she suggesting my key witness was unreliable?

"I don't know," I said. "Coach sounded pretty sure."

"Maybe *he* took it."

I couldn't help but laugh at that.

"Why would Coach want my cap?"

"Maybe he has a nephew with a birthday or something coming up. Don't ask me to think like a thief. Or a man."

Ooh, she was good!

I was done being on the defensive. "You did once say it was the most amazingest cap you'd ever seen . . ."

"You do think I took it! You total creep!"

Suddenly, I had my answer, and it was exactly what I had hoped for: Analisa was completely innocent. It was written all over her face. It was written in her voice. She wasn't acting. She was furious. I had wrongly accused her. Oops.

"No, no," I said. "I *don't—*"

"Don't you?" she asked, then stormed away.

My last friend left in the world—gone, just like that. And all because some idiot stole my cap.

That did it. I was fed up.

I was pretty darn sure where the cap was.

Pretty. Darn. Sure. Or at least pretty darn sure who had stolen it. It was Chase. Or Lance. Or maybe both.

I walked out of the gym into the hall. It was empty and quiet, and the lights were dimmed. I could have easily tiptoed down over to their lockers and . . .

"Enzo?" said a voice behind me.

I screamed. It's startling to be sneaked up on while committing a crime.

"I'm sorry," said the voice. It was Misa. She was smiling a little, but not maliciously. "I didn't mean to startle you."

I clutched at my heart. "You didn't. *[breath]* I just . . . *[breath]* . . . didn't hear . . . *[breath]* you come up . . . *[breath]* behind me."

"I wanted to . . . ," she started to say, then stopped and started over, in a whisper. "I hope you won't tell anyone about this, but I was the cheerleader Coach saw in the locker room."

"You?" I asked.

Just as I'd suspected.

It *was* her I'd suspected, wasn't it? I was getting confused.

"I wanted to put a note in your locker," she said, and handed one to me. It was folded up and had my name written on it in fancy girl writing.

"Go ahead, read it," she said.

I unfolded it and read it silently to myself.

Dear Enzo,
    You probably know that I've crushed on you for a long time.

I stopped reading and looked up at her. She wasn't ugly. The pink streaks were weird, but her eyes were big and bright. So was her smile. I felt uncomfortable noticing all this, so I looked back at the note.

    But now I'm crushing on someone else, someone who likes me back. I just wanted you to know before I let him know. He's a good friend of yours.
                Best wishes,
                Misa

It sort of explained why she had been in the

locker room. I didn't understand why she thought it was important enough, like I cared *who* she crushed on.

"Coach Keller came in before I could put it in your locker, and I got scared and ran." She covered her face with her hands to hide her shame.

So the cheerleader lead was a false one. There were often false leads in crime stories.

I had totally blown it with Analisa over nothing.

"You won't tell anyone, will you?" Misa asked from behind her hands.

I wondered why she had decided to come clean. Maybe she worried one of her cheerleader pals would get in trouble for what she did. Maybe she just felt guilty and needed to confess.

"Can I tell Analisa?" I asked. "Because she thinks I think she did it. Because I kind of accused her of doing it . . ."

Misa lowered her hands. "Oh, that's terrible! And it's my fault! She likes you, too. Not *like* like. She just likes you. I'll straighten it out. I'll tell her the truth. Leave it to me, Enzo."

"Thanks," I said. That was pretty nice of her.

"Say, Misa, did you happen to notice if my cap was in my locker when you went in there?"

Her brow creased. "I didn't get a chance to look in your locker. Because of Coach Keller seeing me . . ."

"Shoot."

"I heard that somebody took it. That's one of the reasons I wanted to tell you about the note. I didn't want you to think I did it."

"Right," I said. "So you're going out with Chase now, huh?"

She blushed. "I guess."

While she was all dreamy, I sprung: "He took my cap, didn't he?"

"No!" she said with a stomp of her foot. "Chase isn't like that! You know that! He wouldn't *steal*!"

I wasn't so sure, and I knew him better than she did. But I said, "I guess you're right. I'm sorry. It's just that it means a lot to me. It has sentimental value."

She softened. "I'm sorry for your loss, Enzo. And I'm sorry about the way I treated you in the hall, too. I kind of have to act that way, you know. The girls expect it."

I kind of understood. It wasn't that different with guys, especially in middle school.

"No problem," I said.

"You want to walk out together?"

I didn't really think this was a good idea, walking with Chase's girlfriend. Besides, I had something I wanted to do. So I made up a lie.

"I forgot, uh . . . something. Something in my gym locker. I better go back. I'll see you later, Misa."

"Bye, Enzo," she said, walking away. "I still think you're cute."

What do you say to that? I said, "Thanks."

When she was out of sight, I broke into Chase's and Lance's lockers.

14.* Notice

I didn't find the cap, but I did find something of value in Lance's locker: his address. It was in his binder. (Big deal. I went through his binder. I was a detective looking for clues. Besides, I'd broken into his locker.)

He didn't live far from Stan. I decided to drop by and do a little spying.

Mom was in the car outside, waiting for me. I'd forgotten about that. I walked over to the driver's side.

"Hey, Lenchito," she said after she rolled down her window. "You ready? How was your day?"

"Perfecto," I lied. "Can I go over to a friend's for a little while? He lives close by."

Mom tightened her lips, which she does when

*Yes, I skipped Chapter 13. If hotels can be superstitious, so can I.

she's irritated. "Okay, but I wish I'd known about this before I drove all the way over here. Next time call, okay?"

"We just decided. Sorry."

I didn't like lying to her, but what else could I do?

"How will you get home?" she asked.

I hadn't thought about that. I really needed to start thinking things through better.

"His mom will drive me," I lied.

She nodded. She believed me. Believed my lies. That didn't feel good.

"Be home by six thirty," she said, then drove away.

If I was going to squeeze in a spy trip to Lance's house and make it home by six thirty, I had to hurry.

So I ran. Soon I saw Lance up ahead with Chase. They were talking and shoving and laughing. Things were obviously real good between them. That's because I was out of the picture. I could imagine how pleased Lance was about that.

I wanted to eavesdrop on them, so I kept a

safe distance. Sometimes, when I thought they saw me, I ducked behind a tree. But they never did.

Chase continued on when they got to Lance's house. Lance went in. His house was one story, which would make spying easier. It was also dark out, which meant I could peek into windows without being seen.

Through the living room window, I watched Lance drop his backpack and jacket onto the floor. Then he went into the kitchen and talked to his mom, who was cooking dinner. I smelled roasting chicken. I was hungry.

Lance then walked out of the kitchen and a couple of seconds later a light came on in a different window. I crept up to it and peeked in. It was his bedroom. He was closing the door behind him. I hoped he wasn't going to change his clothes.

He didn't. He powered up his computer, then fell onto his back on what I assumed was his bed. I couldn't see him after that. I looked at his walls. He had posters tacked up of basketball players and skateboarders. He didn't have any posters signed by any famous basketball players and skateboarders, though.

I did.

I waited for something to happen. I waited for him, specifically, to dig my cap out of some drawer or hiding place and put it on his head and admire himself in the mirror. He didn't.

I got bored. Bored, cold, and hungrier. I began to wonder what I was doing peeking in the windows of the house of a guy I didn't like, and I also began to worry that it might actually be illegal, and that maybe I'd made yet another bonehead decision. There were houses up and down the street on both sides. What if somebody looked out their window and saw me creeping around?

Panicked, I stood up—at the exact time that Lance finally got up from his bed. Wouldn't you know it? We stood there, facing each other in the window. He was a foot or so higher than me. I was wrong about my being able to peek in the windows without being seen. He definitely could see me. He looked surprised at first. Then he grinned down at me.

I turned to run but got tangled up in the little

white metal decorative fence around the bushes and fell onto my face on the lawn. I heard a muted laugh, then heavy footsteps running through the house. I struggled with the idiotic little fence long enough to give Lance time to show up and fire off a couple shots with his cell phone, laughing diabolically the whole time.

"Just wait till these get out," he stopped cackling long enough to say. "Wait till *Killer* sees them!"

At last I freed myself from the mini-fence, and jumped to my feet.

"You stole my cap!" I yelled, pointing my finger at him.

Flash.

"Oh, that was a good one," Lance said. "You look totally insane. One more."

I *was* insane. Totally. I lunged for the camera. He danced out of the way.

Flash.

He tripped me as I sailed by. I landed in the grass.

"Very dignified, Mr. President," Lance said. "Presidential, I'd say."

I got to my feet.

"You have one week to return the cap or I go to the police," I said wildly.

Flash.

"I wish my phone had video," he mumbled loud enough for me to hear. "I knew I should have grabbed my mom's camera . . ."

Suddenly, it struck me: what was I still doing there?

I turned and ran. Into a tree.

Flash.

I got up off the ground (again) and ran away. Fast. This time, I did so without any physical comedy or photo opportunities. I ran and ran and ran. My lungs burned from the running and the cold.

Finally, I had to stop and catch my breath. I dug out my cell, which, of course, was dead.

I started running again. It felt kind of good, actually. I ran most of the way home. When at last I got there, I was totally exhausted and sweaty.

Lupe was standing inside the door, her arms crossed, smiling.

"You're late," she said. "Dinner's over."

I glanced at the girly, silvery, cloud-shaped clock on the mantel: seven fifteen.

"What's it to you?" I asked, and pushed by her.

"They know about your detention."

I froze. "You told them?"

"I told them."

I tried to vaporize her with my eyes. It didn't work.

"They know you lost your cap, too. And that you got dropped from the starting five. I had to give them all the details for it to make sense."

She was having the time of her life. Lucky for her, Dad appeared right then, or it might have been the *end* of her life.

"Can we talk, Enzo?" he asked.

Lupe beamed.

"Sure," I said, firing more visual vaporizing rays at my evil sister. In a perfect world they would have worked.

Dad grounded me for a week. Not because I lost the cap, but because I broke into Chase's duffel, got caught, and got detention. It was like I got punished for getting punished once again. I mean, all I did was unzip my friend's duffel bag to see if the cap he stole was in there. The cap of *mine* he stole. What was wrong with that?

So while I was feeling that there was no justice in the world and wondering if maybe Lupe stole my cap—just to see me suffer—Dad decided it was a good time to drop a bomb.

"I'm thinking of giving notice, Enzo."

"Notice?"

"I might quit my job at Kap." He set his hand on my knee and patted it as if a relative had just died.

I wished it had been only that.

"Stop joking," I said, pushing his hand away. I needed it to be a joke. A very bad joke in extremely bad taste.

"It's just not a good fit," Dad said. "I don't know, maybe I'm just too old . . ."

"NO!" I screamed. "You CAN'T QUIT! Take it back! Now! Take it back!"

"Calm down, Enzo . . ."

"Not till you tell me you're not quitting! Tell me, Dad! You can't quit, Dad! You CAN'T!" I was freaking out, big-time. It was becoming kind of a habit with me.

Dad took a deep breath. I hate when he does that when I'm freaking out. Breathe, that is. If I can't breathe, why should he?

"Listen, Enzo. Kap is too aggressive for my tastes. They go after kids, and I don't hold with that. And they try to run small, independent stores out of business. Like G&W. It's as if they need to be the absolute biggest, coolest, richest athletic company on earth."

"What's wrong with that?" Sometimes I just didn't get the guy.

"I don't need to be a part of that."

"I do!" I wailed, and fell onto my knees.

Dad looked down at me, a little disgusted, I think. I didn't care. My life was coming apart at the seams. *Blowing* apart at the seams. He couldn't take Kap away from me, too.

"That's exactly what I mean," he said calmly. "Look what my working there has done to you."

"What's it done to me?" I asked. "Except make me athletic and popular? Class president? Starter on the basketball team? Big guy on campus?"

"Kap didn't do that."

"Really? Because I sure wasn't like that before Kap hired you."

"Don't be silly. You did that, Enz."

"Get a reality check, Dad. The second that cap hit my head, my life got better. Got great. Amazing! The second it disappeared, my life went down the toilet. I lost everything."

"Not everything."

"Everything."

"You didn't lose me."

"This is no time to get cheesy, Dad. I'm serious. I've got to get that cap back. Can you at least get me another one like it before you quit?" I clasped my hands together like I was praying. I *was* praying. "Pleeeease, Dad? Get me another prototype. Pleeeease?"

"There aren't any more prototypes," he said. "The model's on the market now."

"What? You mean anyone can buy one now?"

"Yes . . ."

"Then I have to get mine back. It's a prototype. It has magic." I looked deep into his eyes. "Magic, Dad!"

"You're being ridiculous."

I went limp, fell onto the couch. All was lost.

"Let it go, Enz. It's just a cap. You have others."

Poor old man. Poor, foolish, naïve old man.

"Don't get into any more trouble because of it. Promise me."

I held up my hand and crossed my fingers.

"Good," he said. "Now come and get some dinner. Your mom saved you a plate."

The next day, I saw my cap on some kid's stupid head, and I pounced on him.

We both got dragged to the principal's office. It wasn't my cap, of course. It wasn't signed by LeBron James. The kid had bought it at the mall. Like Dad said, the model was on the market. That had slipped my mind when I was seized with capmania.

"Do you believe this was behavior befitting a class president?" Ms. Kish asked me.

Befitting?

"No, ma'am," I said.

"I see you got a detention yesterday," she said, flipping through my file.

I had a file.

"Yes, ma'am."

More flipping. "You hadn't been in any trouble this year before that, is that right?"

I nodded.

She set her elbows on my file and leaned toward me. "So what's been different for you lately, Enzo?"

I didn't know if I could trust her. But I decided to risk it. I mean, who wouldn't sympathize with my recent tragedy?

"I lost my cap," I said.

Not "My cap was stolen" or "My magic cap was stolen." I didn't want to give her the chance to think I was nuts.

She leaned back, softened a little. "This cap meant a lot to you?"

"The world," I said.

"And you thought this other boy took it?"

"His cap looked just like mine."

"I see. Sounds like an honest mistake . . ."

"Oh, it totally was!"

"But you certainly handled the situation very poorly. If you suspected the boy had your cap, you should have reported it. You definitely should not have attacked him."

"Oh," I said.

"I'm afraid I'm going to have to give you another lunch detention."

"Are you serious?" Obviously, these adults had me confused with a bad kid. I was a good kid. Who had been wronged. I was a victim.

"I'm afraid so, and I'm going to have to give you a warning as well, regarding the office you hold. If you are given one more disciplinary action this semester, I'm afraid you will have to be impeached."

"Impeached?"

"Removed from office."

It just got better and better.

I was then released back into the school population, where everyone pointed and laughed at me. At least that was how it seemed. I wondered if it was about my jumping the kid with the cap, or if Lance had e-mailed the pictures of me he'd taken all over the school. I later learned it was both, with a little nasty gossip thrown in about me harassing cheerleaders.

I saw another guy wearing my cap, but I didn't attack him. I was learning. The cap was out and catching on. It was probably going to be a hit. Maybe that was why Evan gave the prototype to me in the first place: to get other kids interested in it. I knew Kap gave away free stuff sometimes so kids would wear it around, showing it off, like they were miniature mobile billboards.

Most of us kids weren't that lucky, though, and had to beg our parents to go out and pay for the stuff with the brand names we wanted. That meant the customers (our parents) paid the companies to dress their own kids in ads for the companies.

Evan told me this was how big companies got free advertising. It was something he called "branding." It reminded me of cows, and maybe that's what it was. Kap branded kids instead.

Maybe that's what Dad meant when he said Kap went after kids. Maybe Evan went after me. Maybe that's why he'd invited me on the trip in the first place. To brainwash me. To Kap me. To Kap Stan. To Kap Pasadero. And eventually, the world. The cap was sure cool enough to take over the world.

Those guys at big companies like Kap are so smart!

I guess I should be grateful for everything Kap gave me. I got a great month and a half of traveling with Dad and Evan. I'll never forget it. Ever. I got the cap, which got me elected class president (Was that good? I still hadn't decided . . .) and got me on the basketball team. That was good—at least till it got stolen and I got detention and got dropped from the starting five.

Maybe the cap wasn't really magical at all. Maybe it was just lucky, like a lucky rabbit's foot or a four-leaf clover. When you had the cap, good things happened. When you didn't, bad things happened. That's the thing about luck. There's two kinds: good and bad. There's no in-between.

Before I got the cap, I had a best friend, a dog, and a family. None of them were super great. The best friend wouldn't grow up, the dog was a spaz, and the family was mostly girls. The parents were okay, with okay jobs. We weren't rich, but we weren't poor. I wasn't lucky or unlucky.

After Kap, I still had the spastic dog, only now he wore earrings, and the girls had ruined the house with girl stuff. Dad had the coolest job on the planet, but was considering quitting it. And the best friend? I'd lost him.

Did I have *any* friends?

I sat next to Iris in homeroom to find out.

15. Girl Friend

"Am I total loser now?" I asked Iris.

"Yes, Mr. President," she said.

"And it's because I lost the cap, right?"

"No, sir. It's because you think it's because you lost the cap."

I nodded. I understood that. "I've given up on finding it. I don't care about it anymore."

"Glad to hear it, sir."

"My dad's thinking about quitting his job at Kap."

"So no more caps?"

"I still have plenty." I took off the one I was wearing and stowed it under my seat. "I got another detention."

"I heard."

"Already?"

"Middle school's a fishbowl, sir."

"Did you see the pictures Lance took?"

She snickered.

I glared.

"Sorry, sir."

"Tell me something, Iris," I said. "Why do *you* get out of the bed in the morning?"

She made a serious expression, which made me uncomfortable.

"You should talk to Kai," she said softly.

"Nah. He hates me now. Anyway, he should."

"I bet he doesn't."

I shrugged. "Maybe. I doubt it."

I wasn't going to talk to him.

Coach asked me into his office when I arrived at the gym for P.E. He suspended me from the team for a week, which was two games plus practices, because of Ms. Kish's detention. That's right, a suspension for a detention. I was being punished for being punished. Things were getting out of hand.

"Did you find your cap?" he asked.

"No. But I gave up looking. It's caused me nothing but trouble."

"Good plan."

"The cheerleader you saw was just delivering a note, by the way," I said.

"I see," he said.

"Do I have to tell you her name?" I didn't want to get Misa in trouble.

"No. Let's just put all this behind us."

"After two games," I added. "And practices."

He smiled. "Right. Stay in shape, now. And stay out of trouble."

"Yes, sir," I said, and suited up for P.E.

I'd now told both Coach and Iris I was done thinking about who stole my cap. But I wasn't. I still thought about it all the time. Did I still want it back? Did I still need to know who took it? What did I want? And what didn't I want? I thought about it all during math class instead of paying attention. Here's some of the things I thought:

I wanted to play on the team.

I wanted to be a starter.

I still wanted to hang out with Chase. He was a good guy.

I didn't want to hang out with Lance. He was a bad guy.

I wanted to be a good guy. I wanted to stay out of trouble.

I wanted to hang out with Kai again.

I didn't want Analisa to be mad at me anymore, and wanted to hang out with her, even though she was a girl.

I didn't want the cap back. It caused too much trouble.

I wanted to know who took it.

I didn't want to punish them.

I just wanted to know why they took it.

I wrote my letter of resignation during lunch detention. I gave it to Iris during social studies. I wasn't sure who to hand it to, and I didn't feel like digging into the handbook to find out. This lack of interest in school rules alone was reason enough to show me I wasn't cut out to lead our class.

"Not really your gig, was it?" Iris said when I handed it to her.

"Nope."

"Better to quit than be impeached, I always say."

I'd stopped listening and was checking out Kai, who sat a few seats ahead of me. I stood up and gathered my stuff.

"Where you going?" Iris asked.

"Kai," I said, and walked away.

"Good boy," she said.

"Hey, Kai." I sat in the seat in front of him and twisted around to face him. "I don't have basketball tonight. Want to ride the bus home together?"

He stared at the pencil in his hand. The tip was worn down to the wood.

"Kai?"

Nothing.

I decided to leave him alone, give him time, go to the bus stop later, and see what happened.

Chase was in social studies, too. I moved over and sat behind him. I noticed Kai turn and watch me, and wondered if I'd made another mistake.

Chase acted as if he didn't see me come over.

Or care that I did. I leaned over his shoulder.

"Listen, dude," I whispered. "I'm sorry I got into your duffel. That was totally stupid."

He nodded.

"I'm glad it worked out between you and Misa," I went on. "She'll be class president now, you know. I resigned today."

He didn't turn around, but I could tell this got his attention. He got all perky and alert, like Ink.

"I was thinking we could stop being mad at each other now that you pretty much got everything you dreamed of. What do you say?"

He puffed a laugh, then said, "Maybe."

"But I'm done with Lance. That guy's the biggest jerk I ever met. No offense."

"He's my friend, dude. You should give him a chance. He just thinks you're trying to squeeze him out."

"Maybe," I said. It didn't sound like such a hot idea, but none of my recent ideas had been so hot. "So we're cool?"

He sat there a couple seconds, then he held up his hand and I slapped him five.

"Cool," I said.

Analisa was next.

I found her at cheerleading practice after school. The basketball team was practicing in the gym, too. I didn't want to be seen by Coach, or the guys, or the other cheerleaders, actually. This not wanting to be seen did not make me feel very good about myself.

I stood in the hallway, with my visor pulled down, and tried to catch Analisa's eye. Why did I think the visor would disguise me from everyone except the person I wanted to notice me? I was beginning to realize I wasn't a big thinker and wanted to change that somehow.

Analisa never saw me, and I was going to miss my bus and stand up Kai. I pulled a notebook and a pencil out of my backpack and scribbled a note:

Analisa—
I'm sorry. I know it wasn't you.
I don't care about the stupid cap anymore.
All I care about is our friendship.

I tore this out and wadded it up like the trash it was and stuffed it into my bag. It was too late to take the time to figure out how to write it without sounding like a total dork. Anyway, how would I get it to her? It could wait.

I ran to the bus stop. Kai wasn't there. No one was there. I'd missed the bus.

I sat down, got out my notebook again, and tried writing Analisa another note. And another. And another. Like I said: I'm not a big thinker.

Finally, I came up with a note I could live with:

Analisa,
I'm sorry for thinking you took my cap.
I know you better than that.
I hope you don't hate me.
I'm off the team for a week.
I'm done doing stupid things.
I'm sorry.

Enzo

P.S.-I never found out who stole the
cap but I don't care anymore.

I folded it up, wrote a big *A* on it, and stuffed it into my pocket. Practice would be over in twenty minutes. I thought about sneaking into the girls' locker room and putting it in her locker, then realized that would be a really stupid thing to do, so decided instead to just sit there by the front doors and wait for her to come out.

It was definitely weird that I'd written a note to a girl, especially one asking her to not hate me and telling her I was sorry . . . twice. Weirder was that I was so nervous about giving it to her, and that I was risking having a bunch of girls see me do it. Maybe even a bunch of guys. The *team*, in fact.

Weirdest of all was that I went through with it.

People warned me that middle school changes you. Maybe this was part of what they meant. I'd spent my whole life steering clear of girls—not an easy thing to do in my house. Maybe it was the four sisters who soured me so much on the whole girl thing in the first place. Maybe that wasn't fair. Maybe there was a difference between sisters and girls. Analisa was different than my sisters. For one thing, she was my age. But there were other things, too.

When I saw the cheerleaders walking toward the glass doors, I hid in some bushes. They were all there: Analisa, Misa, Mackenzie, and Cassie. My four former suspects. I stepped out of the bushes when they came by. They jumped a little. Cassie jumped the most. She's the jumpiest.

"Hi, squad," I said, pretending I wasn't the big jerk loser they probably thought I'd become.

They paused, more out of surprise and disgust than willingness to listen to me. Cassie just tried to catch her breath. I seized the moment.

"I wanted to apologize for bugging you guys about my stupid cap," I said. I realized I'd just spoiled part of the note I was going to give to Analisa, but shook it off. "It was . . . stupid of me."

Mackenzie groaned and pushed by me.

Cassie said, "You shouldn't jump out of bushes at people." And walked away.

Misa blushed. "That's okay, Enzo."

That left Analisa. She had her hand on her hip and did not smile. But she didn't frown, either.

I fingered the note in my pocket.

"I hope you don't hate me," I said. "I was a real jerk."

"True," she said.

"I knew you didn't take it. *Wouldn't* take it. I was just, like, a total freaky jerk. I'm sorry."

I heard guy voices. The team was heading toward the doors.

"Can we walk?" I asked.

"Because of . . . ?" She pointed at the guys.

I nodded. She rolled her eyes. We walked.

"Do you hate me now?" I asked.

"Yes."

"A lot?"

"Tons."

"I deserve it."

"Did you find out who stole your cap?"

"No, and I don't care anymore."

That took care of more of my note.

"How about which cheerleader was in the locker room?"

I thought of Misa. "That doesn't matter, either. It's just a cap."

"Wow."

"What?"

"LeBron signed it."

"Yeah . . ." I didn't like thinking about that.

"You still have your memories?"

"Right."

"Why weren't you at practice?"

"I got suspended. For a week. Two games. For being stupid. About the cap."

That did it—the note was officially covered. I wouldn't need to give it to her.

"I saw the pictures," she said. "Lance's pictures."

"It wasn't even because of them. I did more stupid stuff than that. I've been outstupiding myself lately. But I'm done. I've decided to smarten up."

She laughed again. "How you getting home?"

"Oh," I said. Stupidly. "I hadn't thought of that."

"I'll ask my mom to give you a ride."

I smiled. "Thanks."

16. Sugar Hiccups on Cheerios

"Did you give notice today?" I asked Dad as we watched a Kings game that night on TV.

"No."

"How come?"

"You asked me not to."

"And that *worked*?"

"I want to make the right decision."

"I can't believe you'd actually walk away from a job at Kap."

"If it was the right thing to do, I would."

"So you think doing the right thing is more important than getting lots of money and cool stuff and hanging with famous people?"

He laughed down in his chest, like he didn't want me to know he was doing it, then said, "I do."

"Interesting," I said. "You shouldn't base your decision on anything I say then."

"No?"

"No. What does the Sisterhood say?"

"They say they'll support my decision."

"Even Lupe?"

"Even Lupe."

"I'm sure Nadine wants you to quit the big, bad corporation."

"She said she wants me to do what's right."

I thought about this for a second. Then I said, "I'll be right back."

I walked down to the basement, to where Nadine's room was. Her door was painted metallic silver. I knocked. I heard footsteps, then the door opened a crack. The music from inside got louder. Music I didn't know. Strange, rumbling music, with a woman's voice wailing in some strange language. Nadine's face appeared in the opening, above mine. She's taller than me. All of my sisters are.

Weeks before, she had bleached her black hair, then dyed it red. It was pulled back from her face by a white elastic headband. She wore bright red lipstick, a silver miniskirt, a purple bikini top with tassels hanging from it, and white, knee-high boots. This was her new look. Desi called it Goth Go-Go. Not sure what the Go-Go part was about, but the outfit's skimpiness made me uncomfortable. It must have made her uncomfortable, too. It was cold in the basement. Especially considering it was November.

"What is it?" she asked. Her lips barely moved when she talked, like she was a ventriloquist, only she didn't have a dummy.

"Can I t-talk to you?" I asked, suddenly nervous.

She looked me up and down, then said, "Sure," and opened the door.

I had not been in her room in ages. A year, maybe two. She'd redecorated it, but not the way the others had done the upstairs. It wasn't girly. It was a shiny, silver cave. The walls and ceiling were painted metallic silver, same as the door. They looked as if they'd been papered in aluminum foil. I felt as if I were standing in a hall of mirrors, except, because the surfaces were bumpy (the basement walls were made of rock, not plaster), the reflections were murky and distorted. This wasn't helped by the room's dim light, which came from one small lamp with a beaded shade and a red bulb.

Stacks of black plastic milk crates filled with records lined the walls, and a stereo, with a turntable, sat on top of one of the shorter stacks. A record spinning on the turntable was churning out the strange rumbling music with the wailing non-English-speaking woman. Nadine was the only person I knew who owned and played vinyl.

She stepped over to the stereo and lowered the volume. No remote for Nadine.

"What's that music?" I asked.

"You like it?"

"Uh . . ."

"You're curious?"

"Uh . . . sure."

"It's the Cocteau Twins."

"Never heard of them."

She nodded, like she didn't think I would have. "They weren't twins and weren't named Cocteau."

"Are they dead?"

"No. Why?"

Oh, maybe because she said *"weren't* twins and *weren't* named Cocteau"? Or because they were on *vinyl*? Or because Nadine listened to them and she mostly listened to old music by old or dead people—people who probably dressed in the same old-fashioned clothes only she wore?

I didn't answer the question. Instead, I asked, "Is she saying 'sugar hiccup on Cheerios'?"

"I don't think so," she said with a little scowl. "I mean, the song *is* called 'Sugar Hiccup,' but I don't think there's anything about Cheerios."

"Is she singing in English?"

"Yeah. Her name's Elizabeth Fraser. She's Scottish actually. Isn't her voice haunting?"

"I can't tell what she's saying."

"That's part of her mystery," Nadine said with a dreamy smile.

"Sugar Hiccup" stopped suddenly and a louder, sort of punk song kicked in so fast I squeaked. Nadine smiled and turned the volume down a bit more. Not all the way down. Obviously, the music was really important to her. I wondered what she would do if someone stole her Cocteau

Twins record. Would she turn to crime, like I did? I mean, it can't be easy to find Cocteau Twins records anymore. Or *any* records . . .

Nadine swayed slightly to the echoey sound of the fast drums, acting sort of zoned out. Drugged out? How would I know? I was getting more uncomfortable. I started edging toward the door.

"What did you want to talk about?" she asked without really focusing on me. "Having trouble at Stan?"

I shrugged.

"I thought you were class president. Basketball star. Girl magnet."

Girl magnet? What a horrible phrase.

"Not so much anymore."

"Fame is fickle," she said, and fluttered her hand like a butterfly. A joke, I guess. One I didn't get. Was she becoming an adult already? She was only fourteen.

"Dad said you told him he should quit his job at Kap," I blurted out.

"*Told* him? No, I didn't *tell* him to stop selling his soul. He came to me and said he didn't feel right working there. I just listened and supported him. It's not easy to do what is right, Enzo. Especially when people offer you a lot of money and perks."

"Perks," I mumbled to myself. Magic caps, for example.

"We should be proud of Dad," Nadine said.

"For what? For quitting?" This went against every guy code I'd ever heard of.

Hey, wait. I quit the student council.

"He's not quitting. He's resigning in protest. He's refusing to support the company on principle."

"I . . . I resigned as president."

"In protest?"

I really wasn't feeling good. No wonder I never visited Nadine's room.

"Not exactly," I said. "I'd just gotten in so much trouble they were about to kick me out, so I thought I'd better quit first."

"Better to resign than get impeached," she said, which was pretty much what Iris had said.

"I was a lousy president. Misa will be better at it. Iris would be even better, but she ran for treasurer instead."

"Wasn't popular enough to run for president, eh? Not pretty enough?"

She knew the answers, so I didn't bother giving them to her.

"This trouble you got in . . . were you rebelling against the system, against things you believed were unjust?"

"No. I was just trying to get back my favorite cap. Someone stole it."

"So you took the law into your own hands?"

"Huh?"

"You broke the law to find the lawbreaker?"

"Oh. Yeah. I did that. Is that bad?"

She didn't answer. Out loud, anyway. Her silence said a lot.

"Well, what would you do? What if someone stole your record?" I pointed at the turntable. "Wouldn't you try to get it back?"

"What would I do? Be sad, I guess. Wonder why someone would do something like that. Look for another copy?"

"There is no other copy of the cap. It was one of a kind. A prototype."

The music ended suddenly. *Phew*. But then it

was quiet in the glowing red foil cave. Which was extremely uncomfortable. I almost asked her to play the record again. Almost.

"Listen, Enzo," she said, in what was clearly an introduction to some big-sisterly advice, which was what I had come for, but which suddenly I really didn't want to hear. So far most of what she'd said made me feel guilty.

"Yes?" I said anyway.

But her serious expression dissolved into a smile, and she said, "Never mind. You'll figure it out."

Why wouldn't anybody just tell me what to do?

She walked over to the stereo, flipped the record, and the scary music returned.

"You want me to tape this for you?" she asked.

Tape? Did people still tape?

"No, thanks," I said, and hustled out of her cave and back into the modern world.

17. New Cap

Kai stood at the bus stop in the morning, wearing a new Kap cap. My Kap cap. Well, one like it. The cap was certainly a hit with my demographic. (That's Evan-speak for kids my age.)

"Nice cap," I said as I approached.

He didn't look at me. Must have been mad because I stood him up. I had thrown him over for a girl, though I wouldn't be telling him that.

"Sorry about yesterday, dude," I said. "I got . . . detained."

"Another detention, huh?"

So he knew about the detentions.

"I tried to make the bus, but missed it."

This seemed to soften him up a little. Enough to look at me at least.

"Where'd you get the cap?" I asked, eyeing it a little sadly. It reminded me of what I lost.

"From my uncle. For my birthday yesterday."

Whoops. Forgot about that. Why didn't he remind me? It was probably a test. I failed it.

"Happy birthday," I said. "Sorry I forgot."

"That's okay. I'll forget yours on July fourteenth."

"Someone stole my cap, you know." I wanted to change the subject. "They took it out of my locker during a pep rally last week."

"I heard. You don't know who took it?"

"No, and I don't care, either. Stupid cap. I got in so much trouble because of it. Trying to get it back, I mean. Now I say, Who cares? It's just a cap. I have other caps. Like this one." I touched the cap I was wearing.

He looked at it. "Yeah." And he smiled a little.

I took that to mean we were friends again. It wasn't like I was expecting some big movie hug or anything. We were real.

"I'm glad you don't care about the cap anymore," he said. "I mean, you're right to let it go. You don't want to carry anger around with you. It eats you up."

"Yeah. I guess so."

"Now that you understand the cap actually brought you lots of bad luck, and you're better off without it, you should probably *thank* the guy who took it, don't you think?"

"I don't know. That might be going a little far . . ."

"Sounds to me like he did you a big favor, I mean."

"Could have been a she."

"No," he said, like he was sure. "It wasn't a girl."

"How do you know?"

"Because I . . ." He looked down. "I took it."

"What?"

"I'm glad you came around on this. That shows a lot of maturity—"

"*You* took it?"

"Remember, you have other caps. Like you said . . ."

Firecrackers popped in my brain. I swear I could smell smoke.

"*You* took it? You snuck into the locker room during the pep rally and stole it? Like some *thief?*"

"No! Not like that at all!"

He looked pretty terrified, which is just what he should have looked. I bet I looked pretty terrifying.

"I didn't sneak into the dumb locker room," he said. "You set it on the bleachers, and it got bumped off after you went to sit with the jocks. I just climbed down and got it."

"Really?" This cooled my anger a little, if for no reason other than that it forced me to stop and think. Did I really drop it? That would mean I never put it in my locker . . .

"I was going to give it to you, but then . . . well . . . I didn't."

"What did you do with it?"

He gulped. "I threw it . . ." He was afraid to finish.

"Kai, where's my cap?"

Instead of answering, he pointed. "Here comes the bus!"

"Where did you throw it, Kai?"

"Can we talk about this later, Enz? The bus is here."

The bus pulled up to the curb and let out a hiss. I hissed, too. At Kai. The doors opened. Kai climbed aboard. I followed him.

He and I (and Lupe) had been riding the bus every morning since school started, but I always sat by myself. That day I practically sat in Kai's lap.

"Where's my cap, Kai?" I demanded.

"I thought you said you didn't care about it anymore," he said, doubling over like his stomach hurt.

"Just tell me *where* you threw it, Kai," I said firmly. "Or do we need to bring the cops into this?"

He shook his head hard. "No! I'll talk. I'll tell you everything."

"Well?"

"I threw it . . ."

"Go on!"

"I threw it . . ."

"Yesss?"

". . . in the boys' bathroom."

"Where in the boys' bathroom? Not in the *garbage* can in the boys' bathroom?"

I said this so loud everyone on the bus turned and looked. The bus driver checked her big, rectangular rearview mirror.

"Everything okay back there?" she called.

"Fine!" Kai called back.

"Why'd you have to throw it in the *garbage*? Why didn't you give it back to me? Or hide it? Was it because ..."

I didn't know how to put it. I was pretty sure he'd done it because he was so mad at me for snubbing him, for pretending I didn't know him.

"It was stupid," he said, looking at the floor of the bus. "I know it. But I kind of believed that the hat was, you know, like *magic*, or something, that it had changed you, and I . . . I wasn't good enough to be your friend anymore."

"Oh," I said.

"So I stuffed it into my backpack. No one saw me do it. They were all too busy watching the pep rally. So I crawled back up and sat down and watched it, too. I was going to try to find you and return it when it was over, but then I thought maybe you might change your mind and be my friend again if you didn't have the cap. You know . . . if you lost your magic and all. Before I knew it, I'd thrown it in the garbage and was running away." He looked up at me. "And now here you are. Like magic."

He smiled this goofy, weak, crooked smile. He looked like he was going to cry. Talk about uncomfortable. Before the tears fell, thankfully, he pulled off his cap and held it out to me.

"You can have this one," he said. "I know it's not the same. It's not autographed by LeBron James. It's not a prototype."

I pushed the cap away.

"Keep it. I'm good. I thought the cap was magic, too, you know. Lucky. I thought it made me popular and good at stuff. But it didn't. It was just a cool cap. And now there are lots of them. Like yours. And before you know it, there'll be some even cooler cap everyone will want."

"Yeah," he said, looking at the cap. "You're probably right." He smiled. "Does that mean you're not mad at me?"

"To be honest, no, I'm still mad. I loved that

cap. LeBron James signed it, and I met him."

Kai shrank down in the seat.

"But I was acting like such a jerk to you I probably deserved it. I'll forget about it if you'll forget what a jerk I was."

"Deal," Kai said, and raised a fist.

I bumped it. And that was totally that.

18. STAN

"You were right," I said to Iris in homeroom. "Kai doesn't hate me."

"Told you so," she said.

I thought about telling her that it was Kai who stole my cap, that he'd thrown it in the garbage, but I decided not to. What good would it do to rat him out? It was between us, no one else. I wouldn't tell anyone. Case closed.

"I'm not going to pretend he doesn't exist anymore," I said.

"Nice of you," Iris said.

"We're friends again."

"Swell."

"By the way, my dad is quitting Kap for good reasons. Nadine says he isn't really quitting—he's resigning in protest. I think I'm going to support his decision."

"Wow," she said, though she didn't sound excited.

"I'll tell you something else. I don't think I resigned as president for good reasons. I think it was a mistake. I shouldn't have quit just because I was in trouble. I should have tried harder. Or tried at all. I wish I hadn't resigned. Oh, well . . ."

"It just so happens"—Iris said in a singsongy voice as she lifted her backpack and fished around inside it—"I never quite got around to submitting your letter of resignation." She pulled a sheet of paper out of her bag. "Here it is! Shall I rip it to shreds, Mr. President?"

"Sweet!" I said, snatching it and tearing it in half, then in half again. It felt good. "You are awesome, Iris!"

Which might have been the first time I'd ever called a girl that. In fact, I'm sure it was.

"So, do you have some new ideas, Mr. President?" Iris asked, a pen and her eyebrows raised, like a reporter.

"Uh . . . no . . . ," I said, thinking, "but I do

have a couple of new advisers who might."

"Really, sir? Advisers? I would love to know their names."

"You'll find out soon enough," I said. Presidentially.

I gathered Kai, Iris, Analisa, and Kai's new friend, Giovanni, for lunch. At first, I gave Analisa props for risking her reputation by sitting with Kai and Gio, but then she had so much fun with them, I realized the props were unnecessary. I liked Gio, too. He was geeky, for sure, but funny, like a character on TV. Not a main character. A funny, smart one.

After lunch we moved to the Student Commons, which we all knew was a cool-kids-only zone, especially Analisa and me, who had been cool kids most of the year. But it was just too cold that day to go outside, so the cool kids were just going to have to deal.

We found a sofa, a chair, and a table, pulled them all together, and sat down. Then I stood up to speak.

"I need you guys to help me be a good president. I need ideas. Direction. The only ideas I've had so far were getting rid of the no-caps-worn-in-school rule—which I no longer care about—and putting an end to nominating class officers on the first day of school.

"I got nominated by a girl who didn't know my name," I said. "And I accepted the nomination, even though I had no idea what being president meant. I only won because Kyla hung all those posters and because I made kids laugh during my speech. That's crazy. We have to do something to stop this from happening again. We can't let people get nominated and elected just because they're cute or funny or popular like me. They need to be smart and dedicated and know the school rules and stuff. Like Iris."

They all agreed it was an issue worth fighting for. Iris said she'd second it if I made a motion at the next class officer meeting. I felt good for the first time since I'd become president, like I might actually do something worthwhile. So I tossed out another idea:

"How about we increase security in the locker

rooms? Maybe surveillance cameras? Armed guards? A lot of people's valuable stuff gets swiped in those locker rooms, you know . . ."

That one didn't go over as well.

I knew I wasn't the big thinker in the group. Mostly, what I brought to the table was my office. Enzo Prezidenzo. I was comfortable with that.

I heard that a good leader needs to be a good listener and surround himself with wise counsel. I heard it from Iris, actually. I had wise counsel. Giovanni, for example, was some sort of genius. And Kai had always been an honor student. I had noticed a connection between weirdness and smartness for a long time, actually. Like Nadine was supersmart, too. And Iris. They couldn't get elected president because of their weirdnesses, but as my advisers, they could get their ideas into action.

"Together we could turn Stan on its ear," Gio said, then gestured in the air like he was setting a newspaper headline. "'Young reformers turn Stan upside down. They call themselves the Nats. 'Stan' upside down.'"

"'Nats' isn't exactly 'Stan' upside down," Analisa said. "More like backward."

"Close enough," Iris said. "I like it. It's like gnats. The bugs. You know, with a *g*? Always buzzing around, getting in your face? That's us."

"All in favor of calling our think tank the Nats, say aye," I said.

"Aye!" said everyone, including Analisa.

The Nats met for lunch every day after that, and plotted our strategies in the Commons. Nasty rumors flew around at first—the class president and the head cheerleader hanging out with losers and nerds—but we ignored them and nothing horrible happened to any of us. No one got terminally ill, or beaten up. I wasn't kicked off the team. Analisa wasn't kicked off the squad. Pretty soon the rumors died. Or at least stopped reaching us. Or mattering to us. Hard to say which.

I got back on the team, and since Chase didn't continue to play as well as he did in the first game, I got put back in the starting five. Chase didn't get mad this time. He and Misa were still going out, and he was happy.

I asked him once why he liked girls so much, and he said, "Dude, it's okay for a guy to like girls. Welcome to the twentieth century!"

"Isn't it the twenty-first century?" I asked.

He laughed. "So welcome to the twenty-first century!"

Then he asked if he and Misa could join the Nats. I said yes. Which really ticked off Lance, because, of course, he had no interest in hanging out with a bunch of "losers and nerds," as he called us.

I tried my best to be nice to the guy, as I told Chase I might do. I didn't like doing it, but no one said being a good guy was easy.

By winter break, we had made some real headway on the Repeal the First-Day Nomination initiative. Our slogan was KNOW BEFORE YOU NOMINATE! The powers that be—the principal, the district head, even the school board president— came to our meetings to set us straight about what we could and (mostly) couldn't do, but we stuck to our guns.

Iris, especially, turned out to be one tough negotiator. She did her homework and would not be outargued. Cassie kept excellent notes. And I did my best to act presidential. I shook hands firmly. I spoke in a deep voice. And I always remembered to take off my cap.

Word got around about us facing off with the big boys (and girls) and the Nats started to become sort of, kind of, almost, well . . . cool. Kids still pointed at us in the Commons, but in a totally different way. Sometimes they came over and gave us high fives. Gio became genuinely popular once everyone found out how funny he was. He ended up having tons of friends. I bet Kai five bucks that Gio would win the presidency in seventh grade, even though, personally, I thought Iris would do a better job.

One hurdle at a time. Maybe one day far in the future a dorky, smart girl could reach higher than treasurer and be elected class president. For now, all the Nats were after was to stop stuck-up boneheads like me from getting elected.

The basketball team won the first three games I started. Not just because of me, of course. Coach really did a great job working with us, turning us into a real team. But I admit, I was playing well. Analisa and Cassie and Misa cheered for me. Kai and Gio and Iris were in the stands. Chase rooted for me from the bench. Nadine was proud of me, mostly because of the Nats and all. I felt confident, even without the cap.

Eventually, I saw the cap for what it was: a cap. It wasn't magic or lucky. It didn't have anything to do with all the good stuff that had happened to me at Stan, and losing it didn't have anything to do with all the bad stuff. I made all the bad stuff happen myself by acting like a nut after the cap disappeared. So I guess that means I made all the good stuff happen, too, doesn't it?

During winter break my mom hosted a Christmas party. We were all allowed to invite friends. I invited the Nats.

Dad invited Evan, even though he'd given notice at Kap. I was surprised he invited him. And I was surprised Evan accepted, considering how fast my had dad quit his job. I thought Evan would be sore. Shows what I know about adults. Practically nothing.

After Evan gave my mom a hug and my dad a knuckle bump, he came into the living room where I was sitting with the Nats. We were all lounging on the pink couch, by the twinkling Christmas tree. Ink was getting up in everyone's laps and faces, but they all seemed to like him okay. He was wearing jingle bell earrings and a red Santa sweater, courtesy of the Sisterhood.

"Enzo, my man!" Evan said, raising his fist for a bump. "How's it going, bro?"

Everyone stopped talking and looked up at this adult, all decked out in Kap gear, including Kap sunglasses. Inside. At night. In December.

Ink growled.

I stood up and answered Evan's bump. "Hi, Evan. I'm good. You?"

"I am excellent. These your buds? Hey, dudes!"

The Nats waved lazily. Except Analisa. She perked up. I think it was dawning on her Evan was my Kap connection, and she was still pretty into Kap.

"Who's your friend?" Iris asked me, squinting at Evan like he was sketchy.

"Guys, this is Evan Stevens. He works for Kap."

"Evan Stevens?" Iris asked.

"I see you're wearing an awesome new Kap cap, bro!" Evan said to Kai.

Kai reached up and touched it.

"That's Kai," I said.

"Hey, Kai," Evan said.

"You gave Enzo his stuff, didn't you?" Analisa asked him. "You took him on that amazing trip last summer?"

"Guilty," Evan said, holding up his hands like he was surrendering to the police. "I tell you what—*En*-zo knows how to *par*-tee!"

Dazed reaction from all. Even from me. Maybe people were right about middle school changing you. Five months earlier I thought Evan was the coolest guy on the planet. Not anymore. Now he seemed like a guy trying too hard to seem cool. And act our age.

Not knowing what else to do, I continued my introductions.

"That's Analisa, and that's Giovanni, and Iris, and Misa, and over there's Chase."

"Giovanni . . . Iris . . . Misa . . . Chase . . . good to

meet you," Evan said, knuckle-bumping the air in their direction instead of bending down to reach them. "You all seem like Kap people to me." He smiled hugely.

Again, uncomfortable silence.

"We're the Nats," Giovanni piped up. "We're a political activism collective. We're not anarchists, though. We're reformists."

Evan clearly had no idea what to do with this.

"Enzo's kind of our leader," Gio went on.

"Our figurehead, more like," Iris added.

"He's class president," Kai said.

"Enzo Prezidenzo!" Misa chimed in.

Evan looked at me, his head tilted. "Is this *so*, Enzo?"

"It's so. I ran for class office." I didn't say "against your advice." It was implied.

"But you *are* involved in athletics?"

"He's a starter on our basketball team," Chase said. "We've won three in a row."

"*Ex*cellent!" Evan said, pumping his fist.

"Chase is on the team, too," I said. "He's real good. He starts sometimes, too."

"Go, Chase!" Evan said. "I like your apparel, dude."

"Thanks," Chase said, looking down at the Kap jersey he was wearing,

I wasn't wearing any Kap.

"I guess I really got the brand out there for you, Ev," I said.

He slapped me on the back. "That's my man! Which is why I brought you this!" He lifted up a gift bag with a Kap logo on it and offered it to me. "Happy Xmas, Enzo Prezidenzo!"

I took the bag, opened it by the handles, and pulled out some tissue paper. Underneath was a cap.

"It's another prototype," Evan said with pride. "The cap won't be on the market till next year, which means, *Enzo scoops America again!*" And he held up his hands as if he expected applause.

Analisa gasped a little. Kai said, "Lucky." Everyone else just gaped.

The cap was just incredible. The logo was holographic. When you tipped the hat an image inside the logo changed from a starry night to a guy slam-dunking a basketball. Not just a guy. LeBron. On the back of the hat was a silk-screened version of his signature, very similar to the one on the back of my old prototype. But not the same.

The others gathered around to see the holographic effect up close.

"Whoooa!" Kai said.

"That is one extraordinary cap," Gio said.

"You sure got that right, Giuseppe," Evan laughed.

"Giovanni," Iris corrected.

"Sorry," Evan said.

"Thanks, Ev," I said.

Iris glared at me. *Don't go down that road again*, the glare meant.

"De nada," Evan said. "It's too bad we won't be doing any more road trips. That last one was amazing."

"The amazingest," I said, though that was a word I'd decided not to use anymore. It was too fifth grade.

"Right! The *amazingest*! I forgot about that!"

"Did you find a replacement for Dad yet?" I

asked, feeling a little jealous and sad. It really had been an amazingly fun trip.

"I did," he said. "A guy from right here in Pasadero. Guy's name is Steve Velador. He has a kid your age, I think."

"Lance!" Chase said with a laugh.

"So you know him?" Evan said.

"We know him," I said.

Evan looked at me. "I guess it'll be your friend Lance then who'll be going on the next amazing Kap trip."

"Oh," I said, my heart sinking.

Chase, Kai, Gio, and Analisa were staring at me, watching me. They got what I was feeling. Disappointment. Jealousy. Plus embarrassment for feeling it in front of them. After all, they'd never gotten to go on a Kap trip at all.

It occurred to me then that I shouldn't take the new prototype. It should go to Lance. He was the new Kap prince, not me. But I didn't want to hurt Evan's feelings. I thought maybe I'd just give it to Lance after the break. But wouldn't Lance tell his dad? or Evan? Yeah, he would.

I decided to lie. Maybe that's not what I should

have done. Maybe I should have been honest and said I didn't want the cap. The truth was, it didn't fit me anymore.

Considering that, what I said wasn't exactly a lie.

I put the cap on my head and pretended I couldn't get it on.

"Aw, man," I said. "It's too small, Ev."

"Really?" he asked.

"Just adjust it," Gio said.

"It's *not* adjustable, kid," Evan said, offended.

"You know," I said, pretending to be disappointed, "you should give it to Lance. His head is smaller than mine."

Iris giggled. I'm sure she'd told herself some joke about Lance's head size compared to his intelligence. But that wasn't what I meant. His head really was small.

Evan took it from me gently. "Dude, you are noble, you know that?"

I was?

"I'm going to fix you up with something else, though," he said. "You just wait and see. It's going to be *sweet*."

"It's okay, Evan. Really. I'm good."

"Toast!" my mom announced from the dining room, and tapped her glass with a fork. She and all the grown-ups were holding flutes full of bubbly golden liquid.

"Time for me to go hang with the adults," Evan said, rolling his eyes. "You guys take care. And don't burn down the school, okay? At least, don't get caught!" And he winked.

We all just gaped at him, not knowing how to respond.

Then he made a gesture like he was shooting us with a pretend pistol and left.

"I think Evan Stevens forgot to grow up," Iris said.

"Lenchito!" Mom called. "Come on! Bring your friends!"

Everyone jumped to their feet.

"Don't get too excited," I said. "It'll just be sparkling apple juice for us."

This didn't stop them in the slightest, which I took to mean it was okay for middle schoolers to still like apple juice.

"'Lenchito'?" Chase asked as we walked to the

kitchen. He nudged me with his shoulder and laughed.

"Yeah," Kai said. "Lenchito!"

Oh, gee, thanks, Mom.

Patrick Jennings

is the author of many books, including the critically acclaimed *Guinea Dog*, *Faith and the Electric Dogs*, *The Beastly Arms*, and *We Can't All Be Rattlesnakes*. He lives in Washington State.

Visit him at www.patrickjennings.com.